Morning

Slanting

I0593623

to the Right

Afrizal Malna

Publication of this book was made possible, in part, with assistance from the LitRI Translation Funding Program of the National Book Committee and the National Agency for Language Development and Books, Ministry of Education and Culture of the Republic of Indonesia.

First published July 2021 by Reading Sideways Press
20 Tennyson Street, Richmond, VIC, 3121, Australia

readingsidewayspress.com
readingsidewayspress@gmail.com

Typeset in Avara and Caudex

National Library of Australia
Cataloguing-in-publication data is available at http://catalogue.nla.gov.au

ISBN 978-0-6482610-9-4

Designed by Amarawati Ayuningtyas

Thank you to Michele Fuller for proofreading the manuscript.

ISBN 978-0-6482610-9-4

9 780648 261094 >

READING   *RSP*

SIDEWAYS PRESS

Urban Imaginaries

C O N T E N T S

Translators' Note

These stories are taken from Afrizal Malna's collection, *Pagi Yang Miring Ke Kanan* (Penerbit Nyala, 2017). Afrizal wrote many of these stories while living in Berlin in 2015 as a fellow of the DAAD Artists-In-Berlin Program. Other stories have been drawn from a period spanning some 25 years. Afrizal is generally reticent to be dogmatic about how a sentence, paragraph or story could be translated. He has a generous belief in reading and translation as creative acts in themselves. As translators, we want to acknowledge the generosity, warmth and friendship afforded to us by Afrizal himself. These have been moments of fun and wide-ranging conversation, collective introspection, shared meals and *bajaj* rides throughout Jakarta. We feel thankful and fortunate that the intimacy of translation has been echoed in our personal encounters with Afrizal. Our translations have been motivated by an effort to more deeply understand Afrizal's short stories and make them available to new readers.

Accusations
of
False
Theatre

He was tall. Sturdy. Would make a convincing actor. And he was an actor. The sleeves of his shirt were always left unbuttoned. He could be found almost every day near Taman Ismail Marzuki: a place where artists often gathered on Jalan Cikini Raya in Jakarta. Few knew his origins. Some said he was from Sumbawa. His gaze was sharp and sparkling. But it was rarely clear what he was gazing at.

He stood in front of the wall of TIM, as though facing a master no longer physically present. His gaze bored sharply into the wall. Flat. A flat surface which always stirred an inexplicable desire in him. An actor only lives and walks within his own body. Without entering a theatre nor performing on a stage, why would anyone believe him to be an actor? But do people know that every moment of every day is a performance? Because we live. Or because we believe we're living.

"I can't exist each day. I also need to not exist," he said coldly to the wall. He groped through his pant pockets and pulled out a handful of cigarette butts he had gathered from the streets. This explained why his pockets smelt much more like an ashtray than his mouth did. He chose his favourite from amongst the pile: Mascot cigarettes. The cigarette butt, already more than half smoked, was lit once more, and he inhaled long and deep. The smoke filtered into his lungs, as though inhaling the breath of the previous person to smoke that cigarette. The day was edging on to two in the afternoon. He wasn't hungry yet or, to be more precise, he was used to ignoring his hunger.

"Frans!" someone called. He was well known at TIM. Frans didn't care. He didn't turn an inch in the direction of the person who called him.

"Is that Frans over there?"

"Frans is not here and doesn't deign to turn his head," another answered, chuckling. Frans continued walking. It was as if the whole world was flat today. There was no one but himself. Or he himself had become flat. Nothing existed. He didn't force anything and didn't want to be forced. He was on holiday from being someone. On holiday from hunger too. His only desires were to smoke and walk.

Frans knew the TIM complex intimately. Almost every day he walked from one building to the next: the Open Theatre, the Art House, Huriah Adam Studio, Roro Mendut Canteen, the Performing Arts Theatre, the Arena Theatre, and the Gallery; all of which have now been demolished to make way for new buildings. He circled these buildings like an animal pacing outside its cage. This was his house, his country, his homeland whose territory was so small. For him, Indonesia didn't exist. Only TIM existed. But there wasn't a single person who believed he was an artist. They'd never seen his works enter the

ACCUSATIONS OF FALSE THEATRE

illustrious world of art.

The cigarette he was inhaling had reached the end of the tobacco. The flame had crept around the filter, turning it yellow. The burnt filter emitted a pungent smell as the cigarette went out. Frans squatted and began scratching the soil with his long fingernails. The extinguished butt was buried in the soil. Frans stood up, as though he'd just completed a daily chore.

"What are you doing, Frans?" an actress from the Small Theatre asked as she passed by. Frans didn't answer. He really felt he was taking a holiday from being someone today. He almost said he was hungry. But the hunger felt by one person can't necessarily be felt by another. Even when it starts to kill you.

"I haven't had a fuck for two months," Frans launched an inadvertent sentence. The actress, who would play the role of Euis in *The Bottomless Well* by Arifin C. Noer, was startled. She stopped and stared at Frans. Was it worth taking offence? Calmly, Frans began opening the zipper of his fly. Before his pants were open, the actress had fled.

Frans faced the wall once more and spat at it.

"Look at that. She's an actor, but she's anti-the-atre and anti-performance. There are no actors. There's no theatre. Performance is buried alive in my underpants," he said to the wall. "How easy it is to live as man, a bastard," he muttered to himself. "And how easy to second-guess a woman's desires". Frans spat on his hands and continued walking. He didn't know why he had to walk, or where to walk to. He only knew about walking, tasting the street corners of life that always gave themselves over to experience. For him, walking wasn't about the radius covered, but the act of walking itself.

At night, Frans slept below the awnings of shop fronts on Jalan Cikini Raya, or behind a cheap hotel in Gondangdia, not too far from TIM. Sometimes he slept beside Jijok, a companion who was also an actor and a vagrant.

The security guards of TIM regarded the two of them as "hobos," not artists. Nearly every time they turned up, something went missing. They were among the most regular spectators to attend theatre, dance or music performances. They had ways and means of entering without tickets. They entered not to watch the performances, but to sleep while the performances were held. There they could rest on soft seats conducive to sleep. Ali Sadikin, the governor of Jakarta at that time, wasn't familiar with them. Because they were considered vagabonds, not artists.

"I don't care!" Frans scoffed. "They want to call me a vagabond, hobo, artist, I don't care! Being a vagabond, in my opinion, is a way of life!" he said to those who ridiculed him. And Frans treated them seriously, even if he knew he was being made an object of ridicule. That object imprinted itself, formed its own narrative every time it encountered a space that could sustain it, and couldn't be erased. Frans found it necessary to protect that object. Like protecting chocolate so that it doesn't melt in the sun. The taste might be the same, but the form has changed.

Frans placed his index finger on his forehead. He made the shape of a pistol and exclaimed: "Bang! Brain, you all know, this brain isn't made from a stack of books. It's made from the dust of the streets. Thinking in the streets is different to thinking in-doors!" The people around him roared with laughter. Marus, a parking attendant at TIM whose face had once been slashed by a knife, approached with short, robotic steps and gave him a cigarette.

"Thank you friend," Frans greeted him, tak-ing the cigarette. He inhaled, his lungs embracing the smoke. "Knowledge is not a museum, but shit drying under the hot sun!" Frans snorted the ciga-rette smoke through his nostrils. He glared sharply ahead. The people laughed.

"Just one cigarette makes you vomit philosophy, Frans," someone snickered. "Just imagine what a whole packet would do. Philosophy would be dead beneath your cigarette smoke."

"Eh, don't think back to front like that. I live under the sun's rays, not in a pack of cigarettes. Look, what can't grow under the sun? You become stupid like that, because you've traded the sun's rays for a neon lamp." Frans threw what remained of his cigarette on the floor. Without a second glance, he left the artists around him as though nothing had happened. As though there was something real-ly important he had to attend to. His shirt sleeves fluttered in the wind as he strode off. His long hair also fluttered, the sun's rays infiltrating his grease plaited hair. Jijok was sitting on a woven mat in the back of the Huriah Adam theater at TIM, where a recently released film was being discussed. Whenever there was a discussion on film, the artists who came were quite different to the usual TIM crowd. Most were film makers, much classier in appearance than theater artists like Frans and Jijok, whose clothes looked as though they'd never been washed. Jijok followed the discussion contentedly. He caught a glimpse of Frans' figure circling the Huriah Adam building through the glass. Frans entered. He stood at the back, rather than sit down like the rest of the audience. The shoes of the audience were piled up by the entrance.

"Film discussion... sit here," whispered Jijok to Frans.

"No. Film is shit! This is just money talking!" said Frans. People turned towards Frans. He didn't care. His wild gaze scanned the room. Then he disappeared again. The discussion ended and the audience left the building, taking their shoes as they went. A young director was confused. The shoes he was searching for were not there. Vanished. Jijok was nervous. The situation could rapidly deteriorate.

The security guards were embarrassed. Here was an eminent young director whose profile was on the rise, and his shoes had gone missing on their watch. The security guards knew what had to be done. They immediately sought out Frans. Between the Performing Arts Theatre, the Arena Theatre, and Huriah Adam, Frans was nonchalantly seated beside a pond. A security guard approached Frans as he sat on a bench with his trousers rolled up. He looked great with the new pair of shoes adorning his feet.

The young director came and saw that the shoes Frans was wearing were indeed his.

"You embarrass me, Frans. How could you have the nerve to help yourself to other people's shoes? You're shamelessly wearing the shoes you stole," the security guard scolded him.

"Hey, don't talk to me like that. Helped myself how?" Frans stood, lifted his trouser legs, displaying the shiny shoes. A few people began to gather around Frans, including the security guard and the shoeless young director.

"Use your eyes. These shoes look much better on my feet than on the feet of that juvenile director," said Frans, gesturing to the director. "Use your brain. If these shoes look better on my feet than on the young director's, then the shoes belong to me! Fool."

The people looking on were perplexed by Frans' defence.

"You're a maniac!" snapped the security guard.

Upon hearing the word "maniac," Frans promptly left the crowd, as though nothing had happened. As though he hadn't just found himself in a precarious situation. The security guard took off in chase.

"You bum!" screamed the security guard.

But the young director quickly took the guard's hand.

"Let him go. I'm prepared for my shoes to remain on his feet," he said. "Everyone can see that those shoes really do look much better on Frans. I'm a defender of beauty. I'm willing for the shoes to end up on his feet. So, this is all sorted. Don't make a fuss of it."

ACCUSATIONS OF FALSE THEATRE

At that moment, Jijok slipped away and chased after Frans.

"You're too much, Frans! Blatantly helping yourself like that. You could've been beaten up by a lot of people just then," said Jijok.

"Ah, you again, Jijok. Your way of thinking sags under false morality. Do you know the meaning of truth? You can't understand the truth if you let your thinking decompose with false morality. As a matter of fact, you don't know how philosophy is used on the streets," said Frans angrily. "That's it. Now you stare dumbfounded as truth stands gallantly before you in new shoes. There's no doubt, like Descartes who you venerate. We're on the streets, not in a house, an artist's studio or a governor's office. We're not busy defending any position or power. There's only the dust of the streets. Just enjoy it, no use mucking about in search of truth."

Jijok spotted two cigarette butts that still had some length in them, picked them up. He gave one to Frans and took one for himself. They lit and inhaled those cigarettes with steady breaths. Their bodies felt as though drifting with the sun's rays.

"So, truth is a pair of stolen shoes," Jijok mused.

"Cool! Look at my feet." Frans bounced, dancing in his new pair of shoes. Jijok took it all in, inhaling his short cigarette. Charmed. A performance that got to the guts of what it is to be human. A soul responsible only to itself; a movement of the body that does not submit to entry and exit doors; a mind that can cast poetry from a heap of rubbish. Everything was unique, nothing the same. And it all happens but once.

13

* * *

Day turned to night. They searched for cardboard to spread as sleeping mats beneath the
awning of a bakery in Cikini. They tried to sleep, but
sleep wouldn't come and save them from wakeful-
ness. The aroma of bread lingered, wafting out from
below the door of the bakery. The aroma mingled
with the smell of petrol fumes and the sewer under
the pavement. The aroma made their hunger scream.

"You've got money, don't you?" asked Jijok.

"What for?"

"I'm famished!"

"Me too, but I'm flat broke."

"Why ask what for if you're completely skint? You
got my hopes up there. I need to eat something,"
continued Jijok.

"Eh, you again. It's hope that makes us hungry.
Enough. Don't act like a spoilt artist or philosopher.
Hunger is an integral part of bodily life."

"I'm sick of hearing you jabber, Frans. It's
bullshit. Hunger is hunger. It's you who's idealising
hunger. You want me to kill myself tonight to prove
that hunger is not a matter for philosophy or art?"
continued Jijok.

Frans fell silent listening to Jijok's rant.

The street by the bakery with its shabby awning
was getting busier. Cars, motorbikes, city busses
passed with increasing frequency. The sun began to
shine. On mornings like these, they had to abandon
their spot below the bakery awning before the bakery opened and they were moved on. Jijok awoke.

14

But Frans wasn't beside him anymore. Jijok arose. Packed up his cardboard sleeping mat, threw it in a trash can. With blurry eyes, he walked in the direction of the TIM complex. He still had three hours to continue sleeping before the security guards would evict him from there too. Jijok went back to sleep without a mat on the cold floor of the Arena Theatre.

He didn't know how long he had slept when Frans arrived carrying two packages of rice for breakfast.

"Eat," said Frans, pressing a package of rice upon Jijok.

"You lied last night, didn't you? You had money," said Jijok.

"Have a look at my feet. I'm wearing my shabby old shoes again. I went to the pawn shop. Sold that young director's shoes. Not bad for a meal."

"Thank you, Frans," said Jijok, stuffing himself. Fried tempe. Stuffed tofu. Sambal. Prawn crackers. Hot, sweet tea. That morning, Jijok was expected at the youth centre for rehearsals. He was the director of a theatre troupe. The troupe had just won best performance at the Youth Theatre Festival held annually by five youth centres in Jakarta. As the winners of the festival, they would now stage their play at a more prestigious venue: the Arena Theater at Taman Ismail Marzuki.

The show was about to begin. This was the first time the theatre troupe would perform in the Arena Theatre. Jijok had showered and was wearing his best clothes. After conveying a few final notes to the actors and stagehands who would deliver the performance, Jijok left the stage. Tonight, the theatre-going public of Jakarta would see him as a director. He planned to be present in the audience, watching the play he had directed. He would enter through the lobby.

With a feeling of confidence, he strode towards the entrance of the building. But the ticket seller detained him.

"You can't come in!" the ticket seller said firmly.

"What do you mean can't come in? I'm directing this performance," answered Jijok.

"You're a thief. Thieves aren't allowed to enter. You can't fool me!" replied the seller.

Jijok was helpless. Evidently he'd failed to carry himself like a director would. In the end, as the performance took place, he stood in front of the building. Unable to watch the performance he himself had directed.

Frans and Jijok returned to lying down under a shop awning. This time they chose a bicycle shop, so as to avoid the aroma of bread that had sent them mad with hunger.

"They wouldn't let me watch the performance I directed," Jijok muttered as they neared sleep.

"I already told you. It's all false. All performances at TIM are fake. The real theatre is here. On top of this cardboard. Under the awning of this shop. On the sidewalks. In the dust... when we fled from the aroma of bread."

"Frans..." continued Jijok. "Frankly, I don't understand what theatre is."

"You're honest. Good. Not like them. Pretending to know what theatre is, but when they're confronted with the truth, running away as though they've just seen a lion. You know, up to now I've been faking craziness. Let them be content with my acting. They wanted me to look like a madman. I obliged. I satisfied their desire. So they know what humanity is, what madness is, what theatre is. But as you know, I'm not mad. Only you understand it. They don't understand. They'll keep looking at me as an object possessed by madness. You know more about theatre than they do. Pretending to make proletarian theatre, what's more. Even though they're just bourgeois morons who resent poverty. Poverty is…"

"That's enough, Frans. This time I'm not hungry," Jijok cut Frans off. "I don't need your sermon. I'm tired now," Jijok hugged his own body. "Tired".

Frans got up and massaged Jijok's feet. Jijok began to relax into Frans' massage. Several images flashed through Jijok's sleepy mind, like snippets of film rapidly alternating. Each snippet released its own distinctive burst of music. All passing over one other, all slicing, like saws cutting at each other, their teeth becoming increasingly sharp. Increasingly deep. Forcing Jijok to enter a bottomless chasm of sleep. Frans noticed that Jijok had fallen asleep, the rhythm of his breath becoming much more regular than in his waking hours.

But Frans continued to massage Jijok's body as though he was still awake.

"I have to apologise to myself, because I've been treating myself like a madman," Frans said to his sleeping companion. He gazed at the street.

Jijok was sound asleep beneath the blanket of a Jakarta night. Frans stood. Left Jijok to his deep sleep. Frans was never seen again. Disappeared. Vanished. Like everything that passes.

5th May, 2015, Berlin

Xezok
Ker
Lubig
Job
Kurlesok

The train station at Washingtonplatz was rather
busy. The summer tourists poured out of the station.
I was a little worried when I picked her up, because
the city train workers often celebrated Labour Day
by going on strike. But it was a beautiful day. The
weather was pleasant and the sun shone brightly.
And the train that brought her from Leiden was
on time. I waved at her after catching sight of her
among the other passengers, and she threw her
sweet smile at me. Her gaze, warm but firm, was
fixed in my direction. The cold Berlin wind rearranged her fair hair. She walked among the other
passengers as if her feet didn't touch the ground.
I helped her with her suitcase. Human beings, it
seemed, were becoming ever busier with their suitcases.

The weather was too beautiful to ignore. The sun
is so venerated in this country of four seasons. As we
left the station, I asked her if she would like a drink
across the street by the river. She ordered a glass of
milk and I ordered a cup of coffee. We enjoyed the
warmth of the sun. The summer tourist boats sailed
back and forth along the Spree River. Before us, the
station building looked like a church made of glass.

As usual, I sat down and smoked, almost motionless. I didn't want to interrupt the gently blowing breeze and the sunlight. But my eyes scanned every corner. People started to join us at the café by the river. A waiter put out some wooden folding chairs and arranged them in a row by the riverbank. Green grass stretched out as a border between the river and the café. The wind carried a song our way: it was *Not About Angels*, by Birdy. Yeah, of course. Who would dream of angels dancing above the river on a day like this?

We began to converse in a language I didn't quite understand. I forced my ears to listen. What kind of language was this? A language that didn't exist. It sounded so strange. The words were like a musical composition consisting of random vowels and consonants. I could only recognize the odd word at the end of a sentence. Besides that, I only heard a meaningless mix of syllables. She attached no particular importance to the words used to finish her sentences, which she almost sung, rather than spoke. Her words bore no relation to the objects before us. Among those words were: *susu* (milk), *hilang* (lost), *rusak* (damaged), shoe... a mixture of Indonesian and English. But sometimes some Teutonic words snuck into our conversation... *danke*.

I tried to follow this weird conversation, the one utilising a non-existent language. I caught some rich expressions, her body movements, the distinctive way her hand brushed aside the hair which fell on her brow. Everything she did looked amazing.

"Lensibmusidf komdesleom sodifmeslap ekamfbainya … *hilang.*" She said the meaningless sentence confidently, as if everything she said was meaningful and that I understood it.

"Sure, we can walk along the river if you like. But your suitcase is pretty heavy," I replied.

As if she understood what I had said, she stood up and left the café table, and walked down the slope to the river's edge. She did it as if it were her first time walking down a slope. After arriving at the river's edge, she watched the tourist boats and let out her unique laugh, as if laughing at one of the most amazing experiences she had ever had. She laughed with her face looking down. Then she walked towards me, before turning back to the river's edge. I enjoyed watching her every move, as if her body was absorbing new experiences: walking down a sloping path, walking back up again, watching those tourist boats and laughing again. She let the wind build invisible walls.

"Here I am," she said. That was the only complete sentence she spoke to me. I'd been enjoying her strange activities for almost two hours while we were at that café.

"Xezok ker lubig job kurlesok … *rusak,*" I said, trying to mimic her language. She lay down on the grass. The tourist boats kept sailing behind her. I gazed at the blue sky, trying not to bother her again.

An old golden retriever with an elegant face and languid steps passed us, its fair, golden fur dangling from its body. Its owner was an old lady. A wooden bicycle passed. Then, some more tourists with suitcases entered the café. I'd finished my coffee.

21

And she had finished her milk. We'd intended to go to my apartment by bus, but since it would've been full of train workers on strike, we walked along the Spree River. The parks alongside the river were radiant in the sunshine. It felt like winter had made people, plants and animals turn inwards, retreating into themselves, only to emerge once the sun had begun to shine. People were as though reborn. Flowers bloomed first before the leaves painted everything with green and the birds started their chirping. People celebrated by sunbathing. Some of them bared their bodies in the park, as if they belonged to the sun.

Before we reached Hansaplast, we entered a bigger park by the river.

"Here I am," she said again.

"Xezok ker lubig job kurlesok … *hilang*," I replied. She smiled. In front of us, a brother and sister walked together. She ran after them, greeting them with a friendly "hi" in her own language. She slipped between them and suddenly held their hands. They laughed. The three of them wandered happily across the park. I walked behind them, carrying her suitcase. And in that weird, sing-song language, I heard her reveal many things. They just smiled.

I was dumbfounded by this. How could they walk hand in hand, admiring each other? But it didn't last long. Half an hour later, the brother shook his hand free from hers and walked ahead of her.

She ran after him, trying to seize his hand again. But he just turned around and pulled his sister's hand from hers. They ran, leaving her behind. She tried to run after them. Feeling hopeless, she turned to me. She almost cried. It seemed she didn't understand why people wouldn't want to walk hand in hand. She couldn't fathom why people wouldn't want to walk together. What made us stay apart, be different?

"Here I am." This time she said it sadly. I held her hand. I sympathized with her, and I also felt sad. But who is the owner of sadness? I asked her to continue walking with me. A duck swam alone in the river. A tourist boat passed. The boat created a wave which disturbed the duck. Again, she laughed as though laughing at one of the most unusual experiences she had ever had. Did someone live inside the body of the duck? Did someone live inside the body of the boat? Did someone live inside the body of the river?

"Here I am," she said to the duck. The same sentence repeated over and over, but in different contexts, and always a new body to live in.

When we finally arrived at the apartment, she looked pretty tired. She took off her clothes before me. *Naked.* It seemed she had no rules that forbade her from taking her clothes off in front of me. Then she took a bath and fell asleep immediately. Meanwhile, I continue to write this short story: the one I never intended to write. As if I was a thief who stole from her. But now she slept so soundly. Does sleep have a story to tell? Perhaps. But I couldn't sneak into her sleep and see what kind of story was running through her mind. What kind of language did someone use while they were sleeping?

23

Maybe she became a flying piece of paper, or the wind which blew above her nose. I have no right to enter this kind of strange imaginary world, and write about something which came from the world of a sleeping person. It was like imagining life after death, when I'd never been dead. Did I experience sleeping more fully than she who was sleeping right now? I didn't know whether there was life in sleep or not, except for those strange dreams. And I didn't know who wrote those dreams. Me? I didn't even write my own dreams. I didn't have the right to claim those dreams as mine.

She had run out of clean clothes. In the morning I helped her wash and dry them. Afterwards, we had our breakfast at Garcia Café, near my apartment on Waldstrasse. Martina, the owner, served us with a constant smile. A coffee for me and a glass of milk for her. This time she behaved differently. She didn't want to sit on a chair, instead choosing to sit in the doorway of a beauty shop next to the café. I let her be. Someone's desires were sometimes too important to disturb. Who gets to decide whether sitting in front of a beauty shop is a good thing to do or not? If somebody is sitting in front of a beauty shop and imagining repairing beauty inside the shop, well that's another matter. Of course, it was another matter. Before leaving the café, she took a cushion that she liked. I was a bit worried. Luckily... yes, luckily, Martina was very kind. She let us borrow it.

On that bright, sunshine-blessed day, we walked to the Museum of Sport at the Olympic Stadium in Berlin. That stadium stood gracefully between two

24

high towers. Adolf Hitler had commissioned the building, and Werner and Walter March were the architects. The building was surrounded by a vast jungle garden. A massive building; like a fortress made of stone. During the Second World War, some parts of it were destroyed. I felt that the building was more a political site than a sports one. A monumental gothic building of politics, which made everyone feel smaller when they stood before it. It was a monument of politics and sport, a storm of representation stored in its 110,000 spectator capacity.

We sat on the park bench and looked at the vast yard before us. She ate some chocolate we had brought from the apartment while I finished a cigarette I'd rolled at home especially for this trip. The sun was getting hotter. We walked back towards the majestic building, each brick and corner so carefully quantified and calculated. But then her strange behavior started again. She walked aimlessly. Sometimes she moved forwards and then backwards again. Sometimes she moved her feet sideways across the gravel. Or, squatting, she would pick up pieces of gravel and move them somewhere else. Like she was trying to differentiate between the textures of the sandy path, the gravel path and the grassy path.

I envied her of course. How good it would be to walk without any compulsion forcing us towards something. Walking without a concept of direction, enjoying every moment that came to us, like she did. Now she stared at her feet. How afraid they were to walk upon the sand, as if that sandy path would collapse and she would drown if she stepped on it. Then she shrugged her shoulders, quivered. Such fear didn't look frightening. Walked backwards. Alas, she didn't even consider me a destination to walk towards. I started to feel unsure. Should I leave her and finish my plan, which was to visit the museum of sports in the stadium? To observe the greatness of the human body, the bodies of victory and the bodies of defeat loaded with advertisements? Or should I follow her? If I did, then she would be the destination.

After wandering around and following a winding road we finally stepped inside the sports museum. But it was being renovated. What else could we do? This time regret had no place to stay. Almost all of the museum collections were kept in another room. So we decided to play a ball game inside the renovated museum instead. The construction workers ignored us. We played a game with no rules at all. We used our feet to kick and our hands to throw. Kicking and throwing. Those two words made me want to laugh. But she laughed more and more every time she watched the ball pass her body and roll behind her. Then she ran, picked up the ball and threw it at me. Both of us had become part of the museum collection while it was being renovated.

"Bjeg bjek klukluk zeg ro ... *fuck*." She let out a big breathy sound on the last word. I don't know where she got the word 'fuck' from. She seemed to like collecting words and putting them at the end of meaningless sentences. For me, her actions were a

26

way of fighting the customs that dominated many cities. Cities produced by a big factory.

"Klak mom o mo we zuko laku ...*wunderbar*," I replied.

She laughed. I was busy finding a way to stop this futile ball game. I was starting to feel bored and useless. She experienced no such feeling. She had no compulsion to treat time as a measurable thing. That's why she never felt boredom and futility. It feels so hard to free oneself from this kind of burden. I still felt chained by this burden. For all the confusion I had to deal with today, I had a feeling that smoking would be more interesting than continuing to play with the ball. She gave me all of her beauty so I didn't have to ponder these ridiculous questions about what human beings do.

In the evening we parted. She had a dinner invitation with a friend at Kottbusser Tor, and I had dinner with some artists and poets at Uhlandstrasse. They were artists and poets who still believed in searching, constructing concepts, or doing research for their work. Meanwhile, I felt as if I was still attached to her, even though we were apart. She didn't exist within all of this. She didn't exist in the searching, the construction of concepts, the research. She only existed in the moment, knowing and savouring that moment for herself alone. Not for work which would be presented to others at some later date.

"What kind of a night is she having? What's happening to her now?" I thought. I couldn't imagine what was actually taking place during her dinner. A dinner was just an old ritual, a set of rules, chit chat, where some meals would suit personal tastes, and some wouldn't. Later I learnt that she had begun playing up, finally losing her temper, pressing light switches in the dining room. The lights went on and off and on again. She made the music stop and start. She pressed the buttons on her phone, contacting all the numbers kept in it. She rearranged the dishes at the table. The dinner ended with an unstoppable fuss.

Before it becomes a mystery short story, this short story of mine, let me introduce her.

Her name: Cahaya (Light). She is two years and one month old. She came to Berlin, from Leiden, with her parents, to pay me a visit. Cahaya, this little girl, was so adept at capturing my attention that I couldn't focus on anything else.

I went back to my apartment at 10pm. Inside the apartment I saw Cahaya and her parents asleep. Human beings who were tired from a long journey. I kept writing this short story until I no longer knew when I had fallen asleep and when I had written it.

In the morning, I woke up and found myself amid a scattered jumble of colourful paper in the middle of my apartment. On that jumbled paper were doodles by Cahaya. I didn't know whether I ought to walk tip toe, or let the wind lift me out through the windows, to pursue the light (cahaya).

21st May, 2015, Berlin

A Ruler
to
Measure
Shadows

For him, winter was like the fish hidden within the
paintings of Gerhard Richter, the German painter
who often came into his head when winter arrived.
Creating many colours only to hide them again beneath the sweep of another colour. Colours created
as if to resist or give a warm glow to the grey-whites
of winter.

Jürg, a postman who collected photos of the
Pope, tried to submerse his body in the warm air of
the train's heater. His whole body worked to guard
an inner feeling of warmth. To gather it in as tightly
as possible so the warm feeling wouldn't fall out.
So the cold wind wouldn't make a home within his
body. He moved his fingers, wrapped in thick woolen
gloves. Outside the train window, the snow was
transforming the map, confusing his sense of direction and his understanding of where he was in this
city swaddled in white.

He got off the train with hurried steps. His body
left Bahnhof Platz with quick movements, so that it
wouldn't feel the winter wind stalking him. Jürg kept
striding past Neuengasse in Bern. Past the various
shops and cafés that promised a different warmth.
The warmth of Swiss Francs. A busker played music

from glass bottles, jars and wine glasses. As if the sound was driving the city trams that passed below taut cables. The church bells were ringing from Münster Church in Münstergasse, their sound like the past reverberating from gothic halls.

He turned onto Rathausgasse and stopped in front of Schlachthaus Theater Bern. Fixing the position of the collar on his long coat, brushing snow flakes from its shoulders. Jürg pulled out a cigarette and lit it. Cigarette smoke filled his lungs, evoking memories of the addresses he had passed while delivering letters from various countries. He stood in front of the door to the theatre building. An old building that never changed. A building as if never crossed by time, reminding him of a performance that had ended 21 years ago: *Migration Aus Dem Wohnzimmer*, 24 – 25 May, 1993.

"21 years?" He sighed, feeling the warm air escape his body. He still kept a catalogue from the performance in his bag. His wife had found it on a trip to Solo, at the home of Halim HD, an Indonesian friend of theirs. A catalogue with black and white graphics. A picture of a comb, a glass and a telephone. Almost like a café menu. He pulled out the catalogue, flipping through it. Two actors in the performance had since died. The scenographer had also died. Jürg continued exhaling through his mouth, as if there existed a tunnel to another world within his throat, between his lungs and the cold wind outside. A tunnel made by the exhalation of breath.

The performance 21 years ago seemed to still be playing, without an audience, without tickets.

A performance from winter that always left him feeling lost, wherever he was. A performance of frozen bicycles that had been left not far from the theatre building. The light fell from street lamps as though also frozen. He felt as if he could hold the frozen light. There was no audience, no tickets, not even a stage. Again, he tried to convince himself that the performance continued despite ending 21 years ago. A performance that narrowed the movement of time, restricted the cold air and the repeated failure to find actors.

"Jürg!" A woman suddenly called his name.

"Kathi!" he greeted her.

They hugged each other. Jürg watched his hands clasp Kathi's shoulders, as if the hands no longer belonged to his body, before removing them.

"You haven't changed in 21 years," said Kathi.

"You haven't changed either, just like this theatre," Jürg replied.

Kathi looked at the theatre, a morgue of time. Nailed to the memories brought on by cold wind. Jürg pressed her hands. "How've you been?" he asked.

Kathi had spent time in hospital on several occasions due to depression. She was a reporter who had been sent to Kuwait in 1992 to cover the first Gulf War. She'd returned to Bern after less than a month. Since then she was frequently in and out of mental wards. A piece of graffiti: "Amis Raus!" (Americans out!), written in crooked letters on the wall of the St Marien church, often haunted her. A protest against America's role in the Gulf War. "I'm finally better, perhaps," Kathi answered. "But the people around me. You know about this, don't you? I'm gone, Jürg. Forget it. Only a handful of people accept me, like you..." Kathi bit her cheeks as she reached the end of her sentence.

Jürg nodded and hugged Kathi again. "Kathi, you're a reporter who takes portraits from within," he whispered in her ear. "They don't understand a camera like that."

They continued walking, passing Zentrum Nord on the way to their friend Bot's apartment. Bot had invited them over for dinner. He was a painter who only painted exterior and wooden walls. The three of them had met in front of this same theatre 21 years ago. Jürg was delivering a letter to a director who worked in the theatre, Bot was painting a shabby wall inside it, and Kathi was covering the performance that was about to take place there.

"What are you doing these days?" asked Jürg.

"Writing a novel that was once written by another person," Kathi answered.

Jürg was taken aback. "Writing a novel that was once written by another person? You're amazing, Kathi!"

"Yeah, that's my way of reading a novel. As if I myself am the one writing it. What's the difference between writing and reading?" Kathy tried to explain herself, moving her hands continually: "I can feel the temperature of every sentence when I rewrite a novel. And what've you been doing, Jürg?"

"I, as you know, am still collecting photos of the Pope across the ages," Jürg replied. "I put the photos in glass jars. I arrange the jars neatly on my bookshelf".

"Wonderful!" Kathi chirped.

In front of a café, they stopped. They saw one of the actors from the performance of *Migration aus dem Wohnzimmer*, who was performing a scene from 21 years ago. The actor stood wrapped in a Pope costume. A costume that looked like a building, his body the central pillar. The actor was reciting an excerpt from a Vera Filler poem:

> *he is the one you've never seen*
> *wherever you go,*
> *or, if he is in fact here,*
> *somehow I still feel his absence.*

The actor recited the excerpt from the Vera Filler poem while leaning over a dining table, slurping up spaghetti. The spaghetti continued to slip through his lips as though it would never end. At the same time, Vera Filler's poetry exited his mouth, as if peeling off the layers of time blanketing the café walls. Jürg suddenly felt as though he was being strangled by the address of a letter he was yet to deliver. A letter for someone who never existed.

Kathi tugged at Jürg's sleeve, signaling for them to continue on their way. They crossed a bridge over the Aare River. The river, usually clear like a swimming pool and flowing swiftly, was now entirely frozen over. People would twirl along its surface, dancing the white-grey winter. The deep snow had almost reached the windowpane of Bot's apartment. The apartment was small with a simple kitchen. Jürg and Kathi sat at an elongated table covered with a white cloth. Knives rested in a glass in the center of the table. The only point of focus in the kitchen. The rest was merely appliances and white walls.

Bot welcomed them both warmly. They all hugged. Patted each other on the shoulders. "A shivering cold winter," Bot said, as if to himself.

They were welcomed with a bowl of hot mushroom soup. The soft smell of cheese inundated the room. And bread toasted until crispy. Bot brought over a green salad. He had prepared and cooked each dish with care. The aromas filling the dining room added to the flavour of the food they ate.

"Look at our bodies, we're getting old," Bot said, tensing his entire body as if it was escaping him. "And none of us have children." He looked at Jürg: "How is your wife?"

"My wife sends her apologies. Her tropical body finds it quite hard to get out in winter. She's also busy translating old Malay literature into German. Language is strange, the texts are like little flowers hidden in the bush. You have to enter the bush to see the flowers," answered Jürg.

"I don't know the Malay language at all," replied Bot.

"There are many languages we don't know. We also don't know how many languages have been lost. No longer spoken," continued Jürg.

"Languages that have killed themselves or been killed, huh?" Kathi joined the conversation.

"They are dying, and we can't help them. Work,

the kind your wife does, translating between languages, perhaps helps them save each other," Bot spoke, holding his stomach.

"What's wrong with your stomach?" asked Kathi.

"Forget about it," said Bot. "Imagine, this is an old stomach, nearly 61 years old. Compare this stomach with the number of buckets we've used in our lifetimes. How many buckets have we broken over these 61 years," answered Bot. "Jürg, look at Kathi, do you still remember? She was so young, 21 years ago. A camera always hanging from her shoulders, at the ready."

"Yes, she was like a girl from another time." Jürg agreed.

"Of course. At that time I always wore second-hand clothes, handed down from my grandmother. Now I prefer wearing my mother's old clothes." Kathi explained.

"You're smuggling the past into the present, Kathi," Bot laughed.

"I feel comfortable with this way of living," Kathi shrugged, took out a pouch of tobacco, rolled a cigarette and began to suck it. "It means tomorrow doesn't become too special. What's so great about tomorrow, when hope so often makes us feel an absence?"

Bot smacked his forehead. "I like this opinion of yours, Kathi," he exclaimed. "My aspiration is to die in a state of bankruptcy."

"Bankrupt?" Jürg asked.

"Yeah, bankrupt. I have worked as a painter. A job that makes me happy. I sell something tangible.

Measurable. But even so, every time I paint, I feel like I am painting change." Bot paused. "Whenever I feel this, I want to kill myself. My clients don't really purchase what I paint, but rather this change that occurs."

"You really feel that bad?" asked Kathi.

"Maybe I'm exaggerating. But behind all the painting, it's as though I've lost a ruler to measure the shadows." Bot fell silent. Kathi and Jürg joined him in silence. Bot stood up, brought back two bottles of wine, white and red. The two bottles held memories for Jürg, who at that moment looked very happy. His joyful face suddenly sank as he fixed his gaze on the two wine bottles, which were like an eternal couple never to be separated.

"I always open two wines at once for my friends," Bot said.

Jürg's gaze remained fixed. The memory of wine passed through him, as if he were photocopying its aroma. Bot turned on the CD player. The song *Royals* by Lorde began to play, like the rhythm of synchronized shoulder patting under layers of snow. Outside, the snow began to touch the white window frame. Kathi took out her camera, took a photo of the white window, with the images of various dining knives in the centre of the table forming a back-drop. The focus blurred. Knives and white windows. Then glasses, two bottles of wine, and three friends outside of the frame. The click of the camera button as though the three of them had been photographed by silence.

Morning sun disappeared over winter. Jürg

awoke. His wife lay reclined by his side. Sleep no longer welcomed him. His wife was still naked. The heater had made their room hotter and hotter, until his wife had flung off the blanket, letting her naked body feel the warm air radiating from the heater.

Jürg looked at his wife's vagina. A hole that perhaps held another universe within it. A hole that always made men like himself feel lonely. A hole that sometimes made him ask, how many thousands of letters had he delivered to the people who must receive them? What would happen if the letters never reached them?

Jürg got out of bed. He was also naked. He grabbed a pair of underpants and put on some pyjamas. He left the bedroom after covering his wife's naked body with the blanket. He kissed her forehead. A woman from a far away country, who had suddenly become his wife and lived with him for almost 20 years. Time was like a shadow that could no longer be measured.

Kathi pulled back her blanket. There was nobody else in the bed. She had only ever seen the naked body of one other man. That man was her father, drunk. Since then, male bodies were like a missing address to her. Part of her teenage years were spent at a school for prospective monks, where she had studied literature. She finally left that school, instead searching for God's shadow in photography. A well taken photo can produce a shadow outside the space of the photo itself. How scared she was of losing that shadow, the only thing that had motivated her to enter the dark tunnels of life.

Kathi had suspected the camera could become a new church for her. And that church had collapsed when she covered the Gulf War. The world of shadows she had chased was torn apart. Her soul was shaken. Her father took her to a hospital. That's when Kathi felt how the so-called "soul," the glorified soul, could make the body extremely sick. The medicine they gave her killed every feeling in her body, those feelings like the eyes of others. She was subjected to electric shocks, hypnosis.

A shadow that had existed outside of herself, suddenly became part of her. The shock of the Gulf War had thrown her into the world of shadows. But the treatment she received at the hospital destroyed those shadows again. "Someday, these shadows will die," Kathi often worried as she thought of the sun that sank behind tall buildings, lights that illuminated every corner, and virtual spaces like the internet that made humanity lose track of its own shadow.

Kathi left her room to make herself a cup of coffee. She enjoyed every detail of the shadow of the teaspoon, a small spoon that occasionally touched the walls of the cup, as she added a little sugar. Kathi got up to enter her studio with the cup of coffee in her hand. Some of her photos were still plastered to the wall. A photo of a statue of Lenin's head being removed from its body as the Berlin Wall fell. She had travelled to Berlin to capture the moment Lenin's statue was demolished, at that time an important icon in East Berlin.

The rest of the photos contained many unknown

people. Who were they? Why was I taking portraits of people I didn't know and allowing them to become part of my life, thought Kathi as she stared at the photos. How to make those photos take on their own life? By sending the photos to these people? But I don't know who they are, much less their addresses. With an exhibition of the photos? What's the value of these photos? Time that has lost its continuity and order?

Kathi tried to get out of those photos stuck to the wall, to transfer her gaze to the blank white wall beside it. What was there to see on that blank white wall? A border, perhaps. A border that produced an immeasurable shadow between the blank white of the wall and the photos beside it.

Bot took a roller soaked in paint, aimed it at the wall to continue painting. His movements suddenly stopped. He saw the difference between the unpainted part of the wall and the part that had been painted. If he continued working, he would close off, cover up what came before with what came after. A wall founded on layers, continually hiding what came before. Enclosure upon enclosure.

Bot stood, quiet. The paint on the roller began to drip. The smell of paint repeatedly swept over his nose. Imagining enclosure upon enclosure made his body stop. He didn't want to move again. The layers that enclosed the wall suddenly began to move, began to roll over each other. He watched the layers float between the smell of paint, cement, sand, earth and wire.

Bot released the roller, placed it in the paint

39

tub below. He cried, thinking of how each layer enclosed the one beneath it. Tears that could not be painted over, whatever the colour. Tears that did not enclose his shadow. The shadow of those tears dripped onto the wet paint.

Dinner wasn't over. None of them knew how to end it. Jürg opened his bag, opened a letter addressed to someone who had never existed. But their address did exist. The address was clear. The name was not in the government registers. Jürg never gave up, he looked for the name on the internet. But the person had never existed. Yet Jürg remained confident that the person really did exist. He continued to hold onto the letter. It allowed him to retain his hope that one day, somehow, he'd meet that person.

Bot and Kathi stared at the letter. The letter was addressed to a director who was employed at Schlachthaus Theater Bern, 21 years ago. Then Bot told a story about a poet who was always walking. He lived only to walk, until one day, one winter, someone found him dead. His corpse was frozen, resting on the frozen surface of the Aare River. It was as though he was alive inside his own corpse.

Bot took a knife and opened the envelope containing the letter. Took it out. They were all startled to discover that the letter was entirely blank. White. Not a word. Kathi closed her eyes. She remembered the actor with the Pope costume who read the poetry of Vera Filler in the café they passed on the way to Bot's apartment.

he is the one you've never seen

40   A RULER TO MEASURE SHADOWS

wherever you go,
or, if he is in fact here,
somehow I still feel his absence.

Jürg sighed upon hearing this. As though he'd consciously held his breath for 21 years. He stared at the blank piece of paper, as though there was indeed writing buried deep inside it. From the kitchen, Bot could be heard washing their dinner plates and glasses. All conversation had abruptly ended, replaced with the sound of water and the scrubbing of dishes. Kathi took the empty letter. Jürg finished the remaining wine, celebrating this feeling, the absence of someone who'd never been a part of their lives. The absence felt real. Kathi took the letter whose contents were nothing.

"I'm going to try to write how this blank piece of paper must be re-written as a blank piece of paper," she said, putting the letter in her bag.

After the dinner, the three companions were left feeling the same thing: that the dinner had never occurred.

Cracked
Sand

Rain falls upon fire. The sound of rain and fire are mixed together, like the sound of a raging river. Together they become a song of love approaching dusk.

Rain doesn't know why fire is red and hot. Fire doesn't know why rain is called rain every time it falls like a creature made of water falling from the sky. Rain and fire say: let wind travel from city to city, bringing the mountain and sea to you, bringing the sky and Earth to you, bringing the whispers of history closer to your ear. They both reject the news broadcast over television that "rain-fire" has fallen in a city.

We are *rain* and *fire*. Not rain-fire.

Rain and fire engage in small talk like this every morning just to entice the wind to visit closed doors in the morning. Sometimes, the wind blows a leaf on a doorstep. And it says, I've never considered how time counts itself every moment, nor given much thought to small accidents, which happen every now and then.

We are rain and fire for your history borne by the wind.

That morning the sky was blue. Just blue. There

were no clouds. Like the curve of a flattened ball. Like a blue dome floating above fog. The wind, which gathers leaves with the limbs they adjoin, a house with the soil on which it stands, sea with its waves, a mountain with its ravines, didn't blow. All that was visible appeared as stiff, immovable images. Nature and life appeared only as two dimensional portraits in a crystal ball.

In Semarang, a woman was giving birth in a 19th century colonial building. It was a building with tall columns, large walls, large windows and a large veranda. It housed the offices of a bank. These colonial buildings were spread throughout that city so close to the sea's edge. Whenever rain fell or the tide was high, they would be flooded. Outside, shadows of hills and mountains stood like natural temples created by an ongoing geological process.

The woman who was giving birth was from a farming family who lived in a village in Bromo, East Java. The woman didn't know why she'd chosen Semarang as the city in which to give birth. She was just fulfilling an inner compulsion to go to Semarang and give birth in an old building which had been converted into a bank.

All the bank staff panicked when they saw a woman suddenly giving birth. It was impossible to take her to a hospital as she just started to give birth while sitting in a chair used by the bank's customers as they waited in line. The woman's legs were spread. She didn't make a sound as her baby left her womb, just bit the palm of her hand until it bled.

The baby was born from its mother's vagina as

though passing through rain and fire. The sound
of a raging river, the singing of love approaching
dusk. The wind blew once more. The baby, a girl,
was promptly named after the waxy flowers of the
Bougainvillea vine: Paper Flower. Her mother didn't
know why that name suddenly appeared in her
mind and why it would be the name of her baby.

The birth startled all the bank staff and
customers, because the baby didn't have a face. Her
face was flat, but nonetheless graceful and beautiful.
Her mouth was on her belly. Both of her eyes were
on her palms, her ears were on her shoulders.
Every part of her body could breathe and smell her
surroundings. The doctors who visited her refused
to pronounce her disabled, because all of her senses
were working perfectly well. It was merely that
their position had changed. The human body was
revolutionised with the birth of Paper Flower.

Her mother took Paper Flower back to her village
in Bromo. Her husband was a simple man of the village who scraped a living renting horses to tourists
and taking them around the desert of Bromo.

Paper Flower grew up in her own world. She
was acutely sensitive towards things of little apparent importance. She could sit for a long time in
her home doing nothing more than gazing at a wall.
Sometimes, she would stare at a wall for as long as
eight hours. Nobody knew what she saw through
those eyes of hers on the palms of her hands. She
lived as though perennially wearing a mask.

She refused to go to school. Every time she was
asked to go to school, she screamed as if witness-

44   CRACKED SAND

ing a fearful apparition. As though everything she saw was not the true reality. Her eyes, on the palms of her hands, always emitted a mechanical sound like that of a camera recording. Those eyes saw two realities at the same time: the visible reality and the hidden reality.

Paper Flower desperately didn't want to go to school. No one knew that every day she was learning a secret language through the hidden reality, the reality only she could perceive. *Fog,* she said, *I am not the pool of water which flows from your water bottles. Tree,* she said, *I don't understand how to love you. History,* she said, *I don't have a cure for your wounds. Love,* she said, *I wonder whether there is a heart made from a new morning which has just bid farewell to the night.*

Everything appeared to her through the prism of this strange dualism. An ever shifting dualism. But those two realities were knitted back together to produce new clothes, and those clothes became love and a prayer for those who wore them.

Every time Paper Flower watched television with her parents, it was as though a ritual were being undertaken, because she watched television with the palms of her hands. Her hands were raised high, like a person in prayer, tracing the movements of the television screen. Every time she watched the news, Paper Flower would say, *that is not the murderer... that is not the corruptor... the wife of that member of parliament has many lovers... there are lots of weapons and money stashed in that house... that's not the person who blew up the hotel.*

45

Paper Flower could, with terrifying exactitude, point to the real perpetrators in news reports on crime, politics and other matters. Her powers made her parents afraid. They were dangerous powers. Powers which could create turmoil. Powers which made her parents wonder: what is a human being, what is life, what is she capable of? Paper Flower's parents tried to disguise her powers from the out-side world.

Rain falls upon fire. Specks of rain and fire separate themselves from rain and fire, dissipat-ing in the air. One is a gathering of transparent drops that suddenly disperse, the other a bright collection of red sparks. The specks of water and fire create their own flowers, like a new year celebrated by ascetics on a mountaintop.

Droplets and sparks dance, breaking up and then reuniting, becoming the singing of love at the end of a night. They paint time like leaves, covering branches and even their own stems as they grow. Every morning, the tree shrouded in leaves greets the sun through its open green canopy. *Earth can become iron or a papaya, but it cannot become a hotel,* she says. *The sea may become a block of ice or fish, but it cannot turn into a TV,* she says. Droplets and sparks dry themselves, like removing water from a body with a towel after bathing.

In Batu Sangkar, West Sumatra, a city with an ancient Minang history, precisely the same thing happened. A colonial building, now used as a school building, received a sudden visitation from a woman about to give birth. The woman was from a simple family which made a living selling clothes in Medan.

The students and teachers at the school panicked upon seeing the woman giving birth. Her legs were spread. She didn't make a sound during labour, but blood dripped from her tongue. The woman endured the pain by biting her tongue. A baby girl was born, passing through her mother's vagina as though passing through the dance of droplets and sparks.

The baby girl had no features. Her face was as flat as the side of a bucket. Just like the baby born in Semarang. She too was named after the waxy flowers of the Bougainvillea vine: Paper Flower.

The baby grew with the grains of time. Her mother's milk dried up, and in its place, time served and fed her. Every time she was thirsty, Paper Flower drank the milk of time. Her spirit and body were acutely sensitive. She grew like a piece of flesh walking without bones.

Upon learning that everyone had a name, Paper Flower tired of human social life. She felt that language did more harm than good. Some words retained both pain and a knife. Paper Flower chose to spend more time alone. She spent most of her time cleaning. Every day she would wash whatever was dirty: dirty clothes, dirty dishes. She even cleaned mouldy roof tiles.

That morning, the sky was blue. Just blue. There were no clouds. Like the curve of a flattened ball. Like a blue dome floating above fog. The wind, which gathers leaves with the limbs they adjoin, a

47   CRACKED SAND

house with the soil on which it stands, sea with its waves, a mountain with its ravines, didn't blow. All that was visible appeared as stiff, immovable images, nature and life appeared only as two dimensional portraits in a crystal ball.

Paper Flower moved her hands above the surface of the water in the wash basin of her home. The water swirled and made waves. Delicately, ever so delicately. The portraits also began to move. Paper Flower could see history in the wash basin. Armadas of ships departing the Maluku Islands carrying spices, sailing through the port of Malaka, life in Sriwijaya, Majapahit and Singosari. The kingdoms of Pajajaran and Mataram.

People who study with time turn into water when they die. Time moves like an elephant planting banyan trees everywhere. And people hunt that elephant and kill it and cut down the banyan trees after they have grown huge. *We kill the elephants and cut down trees so that our family can live*, she said.

Paper Flower read a lot of written history, different to the history unfolding before her in the wash basin. She could trace the steps of history, like entering into a video made by tears and sea foam. The tropical sun made all of history's colours appear yellowish and dusty.

The day may already be night, it may already be morning, it may be approaching mid-morning. Most unfortunate that the watch on my hand is not the counting of the moon and sun. Paper Flower's

48

parents in Medan were nervous because their child spoke Javanese, Arabic, Chinese and Sanskrit, even though no one had ever taught her these languages. At nine years old, Paper Flower could already speak Dutch, Russian, German and English. No one taught her those languages.

Paper Flower's body became a nest of history and languages. She became more and more averse to encountering others. She continued to clean all day. Until, one day she met a river. The river was so clear, it flowed like a river of words. Many languages and histories flowed through the river's body. Language and history became so clear, flowing through that river.

The fish used various languages to sing in that river. The stones used various colours from history in that river. The sand lived amid the melody of gamelan on the riverbed. Artists permitted themselves to go crazy in order to colour life.

Paper Flower felt the pull of the river. Paper Flower felt her body become like rippling water, dripping and leaking into the soil at the edge of the river. Water dripped from her body and leaked into the soil at the river's edge. Time also started to drip, the sky started to drip, trees started to drip, the river started to drip.

People never saw Paper Flower again. Her family looked for her everywhere. It appeared Paper Flower had simply vanished. But whenever anyone caught a fish in that river, the fish would drip until it became water in their hands.

In Yogyakarta... Bandung... Makassar... Den-

49

pasar... Cirebon... Palembang... Solo... Jakarta... Amsterdam... Tokyo and New York, babies were born without faces. They were all born in colonial buildings.

They were all named Paper Flower.

Mosquito Coil from Helminth

1. Receipt for a Pair of Shoes

I find a black dot; a stain, on the receipt for a pair of shoes. The blackness attracts my attention because it's so out of place. Like grime defiling the neatly printed receipt. Why did I think that the black colour wasn't part of the receipt? And why did I refer to it as "grime"?

I've become incredibly sensitive to every word I use to frame this matter. I don't want to get trapped in poorly chosen words. I don't want to use words that will ultimately take me further away from the matter of the black dot on the receipt for the shoes. It's easy to lose track through one's choice of words. And soon after conflict arises and undermines every sentence you use. This is not the realm of language. This is the realm of a receipt for a pair of shoes. Choosing words with which to speak is like choosing between fire and petrol. Oh, why "fire" and "petrol"? Why not "flowers" and "butterflies"?

I'm watching a creature called language being hounded by ferocious wild animals. The creature is trapped. Everywhere's packed. There is nowhere to run. There is no more empty space. People no longer believe empty space exists. If there still really was empty space, it would soon be discovered, and people would flock to it, take control of it, and in doing so transform it into yet another place that is full. Every place has its master. There is no space without identity. And even this creature must finally surrender itself to brutal language to be devoured. Slowly sinking and finally succumbing to death.

But before its final throes, it is momentarily struck by the question: does heaven exist? If it does exist, heaven is surely not language. Language is a kind of hell. There's nobody who can help you escape the snares of language. Even God doesn't teach us how to pray and do good deeds that ensure we won't tumble into the flaming pit of language.

Oh, who has acted carelessly; leaving a drop of black on this receipt paper? The printer couldn't have made such a mistake. Printing is as pure as the door to heaven. The receipt paper is what's dirty, blighted by the black blot on its surface.

Who cares about all this? There's no way I can return to the shop where I bought the shoes and ask them to give me a new receipt. A clean receipt. The shoe salesman will no doubt be baffled and look at me as if I am a headless chook presenting myself at his shop not in search of shoes, but rather to settle the matter of a clean receipt.

"Miss, or, mister, please exchange my receipt for a clean one, one that doesn't have a stain. Please help me."

Ah, such a scene is impossible. It would only embarrass me. But why is it impossible? Why would it embarrass me? Maybe the employee would be fired by their boss, for issuing a receipt with a black dot on it. Why would they reprint the receipt just because of a black dot? It wouldn't happen.

The black dot has brought a flurry of activity into my day. It's as if there's another person who has inserted themselves in me, all because of the black dot on the receipt. Surely the one who's possessed me is the person who dropped the black dot on the receipt. Goddamn, there's an uninvited guest here. Now, I can't even recall what the pair of shoes I just bought look like. If I report this to the owner of the shop, surely they'll sack the salesperson who gave me the unclean receipt. It's also possible they'll look at me as if they were looking at a headless chook who's turned up at their shop, not to buy a pair of shoes, but in search of a clean receipt of purchase. I try to examine myself again. I start thinking maybe I can get to know the person who inserted themselves in me by asking again: can I be so sure that the black dot is in fact black?

Arrgh, what is the colour black? Give me an explanation. How should I formulate what the colour black is? I focus intensely, trying to visualise the colour black. One of the things I can identify is that the colour black is always dark. Dark? Why dark? Isn't the colour black light? If it's dark, surely I wouldn't be able to perceive the dot as black. It's impossible to recognise the colour black as dark. It's impossible to see black in the darkness. Darkness has different eyes, eyes that look, but can't see.

There's something cruel in the way I perceive the colour black. "Something". Why do I frame it like that? Wording like this isn't precise. It's like I'm persuading myself to look for an alternative to everything. The colour black on the paper of the receipt isn't an alternative, is it? It's absolutely on the paper. It was there before I bought the pair of shoes. Then what business do I have in aligning myself with a black dot this afternoon? Crazy, it's already two in the afternoon. Hot and black.

Black has exited paradise, chosen its own path, like Satan straying from the path of God. The colour black refuses to recognise humans as God's most cherished creatures. Death always wears black robes, black hoods, black clothes. The colour black is negative and opposes all other colours. Every colour is terrified of the colour black because of its strong genetics. Every colour that seeks to touch black, and thus feel it, will change and become a different colour. Like thoughts turning into tattered tin cans.

Maybe black is the origin of all colours. Maybe. This life may also be born of the colour black, no? Could be. Or, more specifically, perhaps life is born from the black that accidentally drips from a force that writes using ink. Then the dot is damned for thousands of years, just like us. It can't be freed from the mechanisms of language, because language is the genetics of the force that writes it. And so language forms every little detail of our lives. I'm witnessing how a black stain on the receipt for a pair of shoes opens a new field of language.

I can't comprehend how black arrives one night and alters all the city's colours. The city residents are shocked and amazed when they wake up in the morning, and all the colours of their city have changed.

Goddamn, I understand more and more now why there's a drop of black on the receipt. It's three o'clock and the day is already drawing to an end. My fingers try to feel the black dot. My fingers are like the fingers of a blind person reading emptiness. *Nothingness.* Black can't be explained in a blacker way. My fingers have a different opinion. They're stubborn. I can't follow the direction the blackness will take, nor where it came from and what it's here for. Why is it on that receipt? I've already conveyed my hypothesis that maybe this life began from a black dot that accidentally fell from a power writing with ink. Who cares about hypotheses like this? Shit, what kind of crazy are you?

I shift my attention to the space of my house. I should put the black dot on the receipt away. I can't linger on it. I've got a million and one things to do today. Where should I put it? I'll just put it in the wardrobe. Hmmm, the wardrobe is made of bamboo. In the rainy season it always gets mouldy and starts to smell. The wardrobe belongs to my mother. She's German. Lives by herself in Berlin. She was a psychologist who worked to free people from their traumatic experiences. Now she travels the world with her friends, filling in the days of retirement. This month she's in Mumbai, India. She gets drunk almost every night. *Mmmmm.*

Ah, don't store it in my mother's closet. I want to store it in the book cabinet. Paper with paper, right? Books and a receipt for a pair of shoes. I hurriedly open the door of the book cabinet. The glass has already acquired a thin layer of fog-like mould from the humidity. Inside the cabinet I find that a spider has made a web in one of the books: *Third and Final Continent.* This is a novel by Jhumpa Lahiri, an Indian writer born in London. I would hate it if the spider believed they had written the novel and were now continuing the story. But the receipt is neither a novel nor a book.

Why does this feel so complicated? My mother is German. Simple, practical, doesn't like to throw smiles around without good reason. But this receipt for a pair of shoes isn't German. Eejit, eejit.

It's just a matter of filing a receipt with a black dot on it, right? There's still the desk drawer. It could be stashed under the mattress. Stowed in a bucket. What's the problem? Stuck to the window pane or the mirror is also just fine, and everyone who comes to my house can see the black dot on the receipt for themselves. No problem.

I get the feeling the house is resistant to the receipt being stored within it. Ah, this house feels foreign to me. Even though every morning I mop the floor and clean the windows once a week. Something emboldens me. I put the receipt inside the refrigerator. I'm sure this action has some motive behind it that even I don't understand. Maybe subconsciously I'm hoping to make black ice cubes. Or that all ice becomes black, so that people no longer use the expression "white as snow". Use "black as snow". Maybe I also want to freeze the blackness. I respect each of these dark motives. Behind each dark motive is an unexpectedly long road.

Uh.

Then I sleep, thinking that surely the blackness won't sleep soundly through the night. It will be shivering for sure. If the blackness had fingers, those fingers would without a doubt sting, feel as though something spiky is growing, sensitive and constricted by the cold. Maybe I'm wrong. Maybe the blackness can't sleep because it's busy stirring the entire contents of the refrigerator into a slurry and eating them. Maybe it has left the fridge, gone to find its lover.

The blackness gives me a reason to get up tomorrow. *Another day.* A day full of new temptations, or perhaps new disturbances brought on by the blackness.

In the morning I wake up and find that the blackness is still in the fridge. I examine the contents of the fridge, nothing has changed. I only find shallots and garlic that are sprouting. It's been a month since I touched the white and brownish onions. I feel like every colour exists within this fridge. It hasn't occurred to me until now that I'm freezing every colour in the refrigerator. The blackness is what makes me aware of my dark and grisly motivation to freeze colour. Every painter would grieve if this life was no longer coloured, if in this world every colour died, never to return. Life without colour. I chuckle a little at this thought. There is something that makes me feel unnerved by my unexpected desires, my unexpected thoughts. Black ice drags my concentration away from the everyday matters it ought to be attending to.

Thank you. Thank you. Hello, good morning. Are you well this morning? I hope you are well. I hope you are happy. I hope all of your needs are fulfilled. I hope you have a shower with a feeling of joy nibbling at every corner of your body. I hope the water showers your body like a plant emitting light as water is sprinkled over it and the earth swaddles its roots. Good morning everybody. Good morning. There is no better expression than the phrase good morning used to greet those who pass by. As if in hearty agreement with all the decisions they will make and the work they will do today. Good morning. Hello. Good morning. Who can hear my voice?

There's nobody here. Just me and the black dot on the receipt.

2.   Receipt for a Pair of Shoes

I become frantic. I quickly order a lorry to bring the refrigerator holding the receipt with the black dot into the city. The lorry arrives straight away. I have to offer 350,000 rupiah before the driver will take the fridge into the city centre. I leave with the lorry carrying the refrigerator into the centre of this city that I love: Solo, a city where you can still see trains travel parallel to the main road. Intermittently a train passes, bringing other cities to the centre of Solo.

Five years ago, the city wasn't growing so fast. I like a city that doesn't grow too rapidly. The development of the city and its residents is balanced. The residents don't get left behind by the growth of the city. But now, I'm beginning to think Solo will be no different from cities like Yogyakarta or Semarang. Shopping centres begin to sprout up everywhere: supermarkets, malls, hypermarts, housing developments, unregulated giant billboards crowding public streets. It will no longer be a "village city". I think the majority of Solo residents live in ways that are closer to village culture. This means the city's growth will betray its own residents. Increasingly formalised urban growth will kill off the strength of the informal economy and culture, which, to this day, have given this city, with its characteristic traditional markets, life. Bicycle taxis will become lonely old vehicles.

The White Elephant, the holy animal of the Kasunanan Kartasura Palace under Sultan Pakubuono II, who founded the city after the Palace of Kasunanan was destroyed by the Sunan Kuning and Pangeran Sambernyawa rebellions in the mid-18th century, may lose the city for a second time. A city that once gave its inhabitants a past full of stories: a swamp that was transformed into a city by using a musical instrument, a gong, to block off the water sources that had made it a swamp. They gave the gong the name *Sekar Delima*. And an oral history in which the head of a virgin female dancer also helps to block the water source.

This is a city of music and dance. Gongs resounding as water strikes them. And the dance of a headless woman above a swamp. This is how I always tell the city's story to my friends. They prefer the romance of this macabre tale to the constant rebellions against the Sultan, the anger at how the King and the court were powerless under Dutch rule, and how the Sultan had to ask for permission from the Dutch government just to choose a new king from the eligible princes. Or the uprisings due to scandals within the palace. The palace can be destroyed. The king can be murdered, betrayed, or simply become the puppet of another power. But myths of the White Elephant, the Sekar Delima gong and the swamp can't be killed. They live on in the historical memory of a people with sincere fealty towards their king.

I'm so happy this morning, my friends. Can you feel my happiness? I feel like I want to greet all the city's inhabitants. I feel like they're all my siblings, my best friends and comrades. I feel as if I and all the city's residents are of one blood. But they don't have a refrigerator with a black blotted receipt for a pair of shoes. Only I possess that. Nobody else has one. This is why I must share my joy. I don't care who they are. I'm only concerned with their interest in the contents of the fridge I'm carrying.

Finally, I arrive at my destination. The fridge gets unloaded from the truck and I place it in the middle of a major intersection in the city centre. I'm awe-struck seeing the refrigerator there, surrounded by four big streets, their mouths all opening onto my refrigerator. I imagine the refrigerator as the White Elephant, the sacred animal of the palace credited with discovering the city in the middle of the 18th century. Now the White Elephant no longer gazes down on swamps or Dutch police, but rather petrol powered vehicles roaming the four diverging streets.

59

All eyes within the vehicles, all eyes crossing the street, start to notice the refrigerator. I look for a source of power so the refrigerator can stay on. I get an electricity current from the corpse of a dead dog splayed out on one of the four streets.

I don't care why this dead dog's body emits electricity. Maybe there's still life within that dead body. Maybe there's a life that's not yet prepared to leave, so it's become an electric current. A life that continues to dwell within the corpse. Maybe the life is having a new experience, existing within a dead body, not an alive one. The life within the carcass isn't bringing the corpse back to life, but rather existing as an electricity current.

Now, the refrigerator is on again, powered by the electrical current from the dog's carcass. I open the door of the fridge. The blackness... Oh, the blackness captures all my attention. The onions which grow and sprout within the refrigerator... Ah, plants growing in ice.

People start gathering to see my refrigerator. I'm busy passing around pieces of paper and pens to everyone who arrives so they can write. I ask them one by one to respond to the question "what is black for you?" They all write their answers on scraps of paper. They're happy. They're so happy. The women blush coyly. I don't know why they're blushing. Maybe they each have their own personal experience with the colour black, and until now haven't had a chance to talk about their experiences. They act as if invited to a place outside of their usual daily routines. It's as though I've invited them out of today's routine.

They busy themselves writing. Some write with great concentration. Some smile to themselves. There are giggles. Some talk to their friends boisterously.

Some laugh loudly. Their loud guffaws bring people further and further out of the conditions of the city. They are no longer bothered by traffic jams. They willingly leave their vehicles on the street: motorbikes, pedicabs, cars, buses, bicycles and push carts. Without a second thought they abandon their comprehension of what a road is. The streets have been transformed into a pile of vehicles abandoned by their owners.

Meanwhile, I'm busy dealing with police who are panicking about this transformation. They'll break up my action that has brought the city to a halt. They say my action is political. That my action is a boycott, an effort to paralyse the city, bring it to a grinding halt. The city government could hit me with a 10 year jail sentence.

I say to the police, are you inhuman, are you ghosts? You're completely disinterested in the enthusiasm the residents of your city show for the blackness within the refrigerator. The confidence of the police officers in carrying out their morning routine begins to waver. Finally, even the police join the residents of the city in articulating what exactly the blackness on the piece of paper I've given them is.

After three hours, the pieces of paper are handed in. There's an enormous number of responses. Almost seven thousand pieces of paper containing descriptions of the colour black.

Black is a flower that someone once gave me at my birthday party, although he and I knew there are no black flowers. This is why the black flower is the devil's flower.

Black is the place where my dog plays all day and howls all night.

Black is my mother who died giving birth to me.

61

Black is the one who leads me home when I'm blind drunk.

Black is the voice I often hear within my soul.

Black is used by all people to write, because they're not allowed to write in red ink.

Black is the underpants I'm wearing today. If I read this out now, the entire city will know that I'm wearing black underpants.

Black is my father, angry because I don't like studying.

Black is when I walk along the beach alone at night.

Black is a bird that gets shot as it enters the city.

Black is the boy who got me pregnant.

Black is cool. It would be better if you put the dead dog in your refrigerator, then everyone would understand what black is.

Black is the people in revolt against the nation because they're bored.

Black is the inspection of your ID card, driver's license and rego.

Black is sorcery.

Black is someone who buys a pair of shoes and has a black blot on their receipt of purchase.

Black costs 800 thousand rupiah.

Goddamn, why do they remind me of my responsibility for the black blot on the receipt paper? No doubt this person has read the receipt in the refrigerator. Because the receipt has information about the shoes I bought, including their price of 800 thousand rupiah. I've half a mind to interview them. To ask, what do they want to do today after writing about the colour black?

Ah, I don't want to work today. I want to meet my darling and make love to him. I want to leave my job and live from whatever I can do for myself. Today, I want to go plundering. Making money isn't work. Work should be creating, making work like an artist, not just making money. Money should be made by plunder, after that I can really work, creating. Today, I've got an urge to get pregnant from any man. I don't care who. I just want to feel a foetus growing and filling my womb which has been empty for 30 years. I don't want a frying pan in my womb. I want to have an embryonic baby inside my womb. Today, I just want to wander. I want to live without direction. Today, I don't want to go to school anymore, but learn whatever I like. Learn from a cat how it hunts prey. Learn from a nation how it has ears to hear and legs to move. Learn from a mouse how it nibbles a piece of soap at night. Learn how to buy a pair of shoes that have a black blot on the receipt of purchase. A price of 800,000 rupiah. Find out where I can buy them.

That day the city's residents found a new direction in their lives. As if they each encountered themselves anew.

My action was more successful than I'd anticipated. An action that created an encounter between the people of the city and their own selves. As if they were having a reunion with themselves. They go home with new hopes. The midday sun gushes as if releasing completely new light. The rays penetrate every corner of life like water seeping into cotton.

The sky is like a big painting celebrating the city

residents' emotion at encountering themselves anew.

3.   Reunion with Time in the Bathroom

Morning comes again like a pushcart with a
heavy load. I'm in the bathroom. Sitting on the toilet
looking at the dog carcass. The dog carcass I used
yesterday morning as a power source so the fridge
could stay on throughout the action in the middle of
the city. I've just realised that there is also a black
blot on the dog's corpse. I haven't found a single
wound on the corpse. She died because someone hit
her with a car. Maybe she has internal wounds. I see
there is in fact some dried blood on her cheek. Maybe caused by a fatal kiss from her lover. A kiss that
hurt both parties. Her eyes are closed as if in a deep
sleep. Sleep recording departure.

For a long time I stare with a focus that doesn't
ever leave the carcass. Concentration brings me to
see the dog carcass as silent language. Language
that has just bathed after a deep sleep. Language
that isn't noisy, like a dictionary made of rivers and
rustling leaves. Language only used to read and
understand, not to speak.

The dog corpse begins to tell a story. I don't know
what breed of dog. I'm no dog lover. I just like dog
carcasses.

My body was clean and well maintained, she
said. My master looked after me well. Every day I
was washed and powdered. No flea could sneak into
my soft white fur. Every morning and night I played
with my master. My master always invited me to

64

speak. He told many stories about human behaviour. I was familiar with human matters. My master said humankind is arrogant, because they have seduced God so angels and demons will worship them.

Almost every night my master took me out. Invited me to see the nightlife. All the things humans do at night. Humans distinguish between nighttime and daytime work. Once my master took me just to watch a child who was sleeping deeply through the night. I felt like swallowing the child's head. But my master said, you should never disturb a sleeping creature.

Sleep is a perfect encounter between us and life. Sleep has no colour. No time arrives and grows while we sleep. Sleep is a love that never demands faithfulness and responsibility from us. Sleep is intestines, lungs, heart, blood, conducting a ritual within our bodies and making our bodies into a shrine without a spirit.

Sleep is the death of a loved one whose life evaporates and makes morning dew their dwelling place. Sleep is poetry written by sublime breath.

What's your name? I ask.

Helminth, she answers. Worms that grow in the stomach of humans. I don't know why my master gave me a name like that. But I like to hear it. I like it every time my master calls my name. The name sometimes makes me feel as though I live in the belly of a human, warm, fetid and slimy. Maybe my master had his own reasons for giving me a name like that. I don't get why humans always want to search for meaning. Who knows, my name could mean anything. Everyone's entitled to give it meaning, whether they like me or intend to poison and kill me. Haven't human stomachs swallowed many deaths since they first began to eat? Their bellies are warm graves for all the food they've eaten. Maybe my master used that name to make me a walking tombstone to humanity. Worms that grow in the belly of humans. Ah, my master sure has a distinctive sense of humour about humans.

What is your master's name? I ask.

My master is he who forbade me to disturb sleeping people, she replied. My master often visits the dying, waiting for fate to retrieve them.

He often leads the spirits of the dead toward the places where they will be chosen. Sometimes he uses these spirits to make performances at night. My master is no entertainer, stripping corpses to make a spectacle of the naked dance of the dead.

My master likes to play at the graveyard every night, or invite me to play around the shady frangipani tree. According to my master, every leaf of the frangipani tree holds the story of a person who has died. Frangipani trees are like books that preserve tales of death. My master doesn't like libraries. According to my master, minds have been ceaselessly murdered in libraries throughout human history.

Three hundred years ago I lived as a queen in Egypt. I am the canine incarnation of that Egyptian queen. But I believe I'm the incarnation of a king from China or an ascetic from India, not the incarnation of an Egyptian queen. I'm not the incarnation of the sultan of Java or Bali. When the sultan of

Java or Bali dies, probably they're dead. There's no continuation. They don't reincarnate. I don't know why it's so. I'm only a dog. My face looks more like a king's crown than the breasts of an Egyptian queen.

Time travel for me is our journey to improve our vision of the past, not the future. Because we don't know anything about the future. We only know about the past. The future is a secret hidden in our eyelids. If we think about the future, we're really just reevaluating our vision of the past. History doesn't exist. What exists is a vision that continually changes. We compose the future from scraps of the past that we knit back into new clothes.

According to my owner, humans don't like this idea because humans want to make a different history to give their life meaning. So that they feel they've done many meaningful things throughout their lives. Humans are sad creatures, because they let themselves suffer with tedious burdens like this.

I keep gazing at the dog carcass that's beginning to rot. My legs and arse have gone numb from sitting on the toilet for so long. The dog corpse is like sleep emitting a rotten smell. A foul smelling sleep full of stories. Now I start to question who this corpse in my bathroom is. Is it the dog that has become a fetid carcass, or the world of stories?

Blessed are those who sleep soundly and perfectly encounter themselves. Blessed are those who have ears to hear the sounds arising from the steps of time. Blessed are those who can spend hours in a bathroom with a dog's corpse, and feel the intestines in their stomach begin to move and replace the muscles in their back.

My master blew a prayer into my body by spitting into my mouth every morning and making me swallow it, the dog corpse continued. From this saliva I could feel the loneliness of thousands of years. Loneliness that has endured since the beginning of creation. Loneliness from experiments that produce results whose qualities always change. Saliva from sadness, because of the inability to end, to finish, to be complete, to die, to become nothing. Saliva from those who finally must use time to dance, making a dance from time that flows and knits it together. A dance outside of themselves, who are full of blood, suffering and lies. All my howls at night are prayers to free the barbed wire that has ensnared time within history and ensnares all plans for the future.

Who is your master? The devil?

My body wants to explode. The bathroom also wants to explode. I have talked at length about my master, and you're still not satisfied. Still questioning. Did you not hear all I told you about my master? I could have simply told you my master is the saliva of humanity that every morning entered my mouth, the dog carcass retorts. My arse feels like it's starting to rot, as though I'm sitting on a corpse. I can no longer distinguish between the stench emitted by the dog and the one coming from my arse. The worms that were dancing now enter another hole.

But why is there a black blot on your clean white fur? I ask. The rotten smell coming from the body of the corpse suddenly vanishes. The numb feeling controlling my arse and legs, making me feel like the

MOSQUITO COIL FROM HELMINTH

bathroom floor was growing and chaining my body
to the toilet, also vanishes. My body feels light. I feel
as if I no longer have a body. I feel like the bathroom
and I are no longer different. I am the bathroom.
The bathroom is me. Clear and certain. There's
nothing to doubt. The only things unchanged are the
corpse of the dog and gravity. If gravity is transformed into the bathroom, the dog carcass will float.
Weight loses its meaning and loses a place to remain
as a living creature on the floor.

The blackness is what brought me to my death,
replied the dog corpse. Yesterday I went with my
master to a shoe shop to watch humans buy shoes.
We watched them carefully, witnessing their feet
alternate between the many shoes they tried on.
For a long time we were both in the shoe shop, until
I could hear the heartbeat of the shoe shop assistant
who served every customer like they were serving
a king who had deigned to wear the shoes of that
shoe shop. My master said humans are only special
because throughout the ages they have been com-
mitted to wearing shoes.

Then we left for home. In the street, my master noticed a black blot on my white fur. My master wondered who had dropped the black onto my
white fur. I didn't know. My master had just washed
me before visiting the shoe shop. On the street we
became engrossed in the black spot on my white fur.
My master found it most outrageous, because nothing escapes his observation. My master can uncover
any secret no matter how well hidden. My master
was so preoccupied with the black blot on my white

69

fur that he lost his senses and I walked onto the road and was hit by a truck. I died instantly.

My master was so angry that he couldn't save me. His thousands of years of age had betrayed him. All of his experience and abilities were of no use. The black blot on my white fur had apparently blunted all my master's power.

So even the devil doesn't know the origin of the black blot? I ask.

My master wasn't a devil, the dog retorted. My master was just a writer who once wrote on the corpse of a fisherman who died in his boat, because he didn't have any paper to write on at that moment. My master couldn't possibly write on the body of a fish, because fish bodies are slippery. My master wouldn't let the sentences he writes swim in water. He preferred to write on the corpse of a fisherman before the fisherman was buried by his family.

4. A Project of Memory, Time and Love

I don't think I'll boil rocks for lunch. Since I received the receipt with the black blot for a pair of shoes, I've experienced many unexpected things, and pursued them like a dog following its master. Like this dog who, stooping in the middle of the road not knowing where her master would turn next, is suddenly hit by a vehicle and dies. Helminth, so it is with me too. My encounter with Helminth led me to many things. But in the middle of the road, before I knew what was happening to me, the story suddenly died. The dog carcass no longer told a story. It was as though I had suddenly died young in the middle of a story told by Helminth. I buried her. No way would I put a dog carcass in the fridge.

I don't know who left me in the middle of the road like this, in precisely the same place as my refrigerator action yesterday morning. I buried the dog carcass. But I feel like the dog carcass has buried me by way of its death and its stories that have continued for almost two days now after the incident of the refrigerator action at the intersection.

Helminth had to go through her own death before she could divulge her stories to me. I can't imagine how my acquaintance with Helminth might have gone if we'd known each other earlier, while she was still alive. It's as though an expensive transaction has taken place between Helminth's life and the stories she's experienced to get them to me. She let herself die just so her stories could live on, go their own way.

I should return to the black blot on the paper receipt for the shoes, the beginning of all these events that have led me to Helminth's grave, where I stand now. I don't know what's changed with the black blot. But I keep monitoring it like monitoring time, second by second. For days my eyes haven't strayed from the black blot. I continue this activity intentionally, carefully. My thoughts become increasingly narrow, increasingly focused on the black blot. While concentrating thus, many of my memories and recollections begin to evaporate, falling like autumn leaves. Names, various occurrences, places and times of incidents, all sorts of references begin to disappear from my memory. My thoughts are like a tree that has been left behind by its leaves and is nearing collapse.

The world outside me evaporates like chunks of ice melting under the sting of the summer sun. Like gusts of strong wind eroding dunes in the desert. My thoughts are almost a blank piece of paper. My thoughts seldom command my body to do something. Then I begin to feel that a hook has been released from my knee. It turns out my knee cap has become detached. I see the moment when my legs leave me. I also see the moment when my hands go, leaving my body. Now, I barely move any more, silent beside the black blot. I return to feel 50 years pass through my body. The intestines in my stomach move again, filling my back.

How should I see myself now? A lonely forehead without a living mind. I am moving within a stream, whose minutiae I can feel in great detail, like morning drizzle. Like the sound of someone sweeping with a straw broom. In the current I see my whole body retreating in a naked state, leaving me. That body has become love's property. I cry upon seeing it, seeing the way it's doing something without me.

The black blot has brought me to an understanding of a valley that has awaited my body for 50 years. A valley of time. A valley where love is no longer in question. A valley where my body determines itself. I'm full of emotion seeing it. Good morning my friends. Welcome to the valley of time. I see that my body has made a spring full of colour. Leaves that make colour from everyone who has died. My body moves in a touching way without a mind controlling it. As if dancing. It's like Helminth, worms that grow in the belly of humans. It emits the smell of sunlight. It has evaded my "project of memory" to meet with its own cosmology.

I want to chase it. Hug it, just to hear the conversation between time and love that have met within my body leaving my self. It's like I'm seeing Narcissus who rose from the grave with a robe of water from the pond that killed him, just because he wanted to see his own face reflected in the surface of the pool.

The day is getting on, like a keyhole that will soon close. There's no longer a body that I control or that controls me. Separation from my body is a separation from all the bustle of civilisation.

Call me "Helminth". That's my name. I'm no longer the descendent of anyone. Even though I'm often visited by time, arriving from a hundred years ago as if I have known and experienced it. I'm the product of a rush of flawed recycling. My body has now left me to follow its own path, looking for a different life as flesh that can see and hear. Flesh that refuses to think, precisely because it can see and hear.

One day if we meet again, maybe it will talk of a different dinner. An unusual dinner. I don't know what will happen after that. Maybe it has just become aware of the morning sun, a dawn that fills all its emotions, that makes a different sparkle on the surface of the river, that makes each leaf a small planet in the arrangement of light, after it has

73

MOSQUITO COIL FROM HELMINTH

succeeded in freeing the chains of humanity from its neck.

5. Mosquito Coil Transformation

After the Helminth incident, I can no longer see myself. I can only feel. I no longer need shampoo to keep my hair clean. Now I'm standing on top of a burning mosquito coil. And I see again every story from the dog carcass within the mosquito coil, with its embers that continue to spread as if making footsteps of fire and ash.

In a few moments the glowing embers will reach me too. Will I step away from the mosquito coil before the embers reach me? Or will I let myself become part of what is burnt by the coals that creep forward along the spiral? I don't know whether I will burn. If I burn, who will suffer the smell of smoke coming from my burning self?

Who will be the victim? Who has put me within this burning mosquito coil, made me the spindle supporting the mosquito coil? Who designed mos-quito repellent in coil form?

Outside, the papaya trees and 10 watt neon bulbs on the bamboo gate are making night. In the open drawer, I see a yellowed piece of paper. A paper receipt for a pair of shoes. Perhaps proof of a shoe purchase once made by my in-laws that's been filed away until now. The receipt is dated: March 26, 1954, issued by *The Good Shoe Store*. But there's no black blot on this receipt. My mind moves quickly upon discovering this. I open the receipt for the pair of shoes that I bought two days ago. The receipt has the same date written on it: March 26, 1954.

The date when I bought the pair of shoes two days ago was the 25th of January, 2005. The name of the shop is also the same. *The Good Shoe Store.* I have stepped backwards 51 years. Like the power of time is pressing me back to find something from 51 years ago. And I have travelled there using a mosquito coil. I'm thankful I didn't encounter Sunan Kuning or Pangeran Sambernyowo in the shoe shop.

Now I'm on the final embers, the smallest ring, the centre of the circle, the finish point of the mosquito coil. I see the colours of the walls of my house begin to change, like the colour of skin on a human head. Then hair begins to grow from the walls. Hair that fills the entire walls. Hair that continues to grow. Black curly hair. And wind begins to blow, making the hair dance about.

Suddenly, I'm reminded of a story told about Solo, where the head of a female dancer is used to block a water source so that Solo will no longer be a swamp. Hair that dances. That hair has now filled the walls of my house and begins to suck up the objects within it one by one. Chairs, desk, computer, TV, farewell. Refrigerator, plates, stove, spoons, forks, pans, deep-fryer, farewell. Bed, mattress, wardrobe, clothes, bag, farewell. Bath scoop, bucket, basin, towel, shoes, farewell. Books, newspapers, magazines, saw, hammer, pliers, screwdriver, umbrella, farewell. Soap, scissors, glasses, pillow, farewell. I don't know the meaning of time and humanity without these things.

My house is now clean, as though uninhabited. I feel a line appear from the mosquito coil embers, at their final point, where I stand. A sharp line from an arrow-shaped spool that's used to prevent the mosquito coil from burning any further.

The wind suddenly stops blowing, as though life has stopped. Time has stopped. As if everything is waiting. Waiting for a different life. I begin to understand where I buried Helminth yesterday. I begin to understand that Helminth has returned. Helminth has reincarnated again for the umpteenth time in the cycle of reincarnation she must inhabit. I hear the sound of gamelan and Javanese verse. It sounds like it's coming from the swamp. A hazy picture of a white elephant encircling a large banyan tree. I feel the hair filling the walls begin to absorb me. Embrace me within story-filled fibres. I still have time to see the smallest point of light from the embers of the mosquito coil that continue to burn.

And there, through the foliage of the teak forest. A moment longer and dawn will rise from behind the neck of time.

MOSQUITO COIL FROM HELMINTH

The Ox on the Seabed

The handful of dirt I'd scooped up filled my mouth. The block of ice, carried by the coolie wearing only sacks for shoes, slid off his back and into the drain. The ice broke into fragments and mixed with the rubbish and waste in the drain. A woman shouted "fire!" but abruptly covered her mouth.

The locals had become increasingly tense since rumours began to spread that their houses would be razed. They were also worried about the possibility of fires. Rojie, the man who lived at the end of the lane, had sold his house. Rumour had it he had only made a little bit of money from the sale. His profit was diminished by the debt he had to pay to the owner of the shop behind his house, the same person who bought his house.

City life was developing quickly, making the kampung atmosphere feel increasingly antiquated. One could smell the stench of hard lives: the smell of humans who were hard like iron. People spoke in short sentences and lived in small houses organised in narrow rows. We made our own roofs of zinc and plastic. We made stairs from recycled wood.

Soon after I returned from speaking with the

neighbourhood representative about the price of land, an ox appeared in the kampung. Suddenly the neighbourhood became quiet: neighbourly conversation, music from a tape recorder, commercials on televisions and radios, everything stopped. People came out of their houses, one by one, to look at the ox.

The ox walked slowly around the kampung as if it was familiar with the narrow lanes. There were no grassy fields here, but the ox walked confidently from one lane to the next. No one knew where it came from. Some suggested it should be slaughtered and its meat sold. But the women objected. They felt a certain fondness for the ox. The way it mooed brought back a self-respect that had long been lost in our kampung.

Every day the ox walked gracefully through the kampung's narrow lanes. Sometimes it would stop in front of a kitchen door and watch the women as they cooked. The folds of skin on its neck rippled as it walked, bringing to mind the black clouds that gather before a heavy downpour.

Sometimes the ox would lie down in front of a door, and when night came it would head toward the prayer house. The ox's eyes would close as students recited the Qur'an. The women said that within the ox's eyes was a fresh and translucent spring. And so the ox became part of our kampung. People began to feel that our kampung meant something.

Since the arrival of the ox, we'd become increasingly concerned with cleanliness. We hung more lights in the lanes. Our kampung became clear of rubbish, fresher. We began to behave like one big family. Something indeed had changed. We reacted differently toward the rumours that our kampung would be razed. Previously, we were only concerned with being paid out at a good price; now, we started to regret that our newly beloved kampung would be lost. Our kampung wasn't just the place where we lived. It also held our past, our memories and emotions.

Our kampung had given birth to memories of people and the great rainstorms that besieged us durings blackouts. Trees had been felled to build new huts. Only one tree was allowed to remain in our kampung. It was an old tree, and no one knew its exact age. But we all knew that it was to be protected. It was sacred. It was where our ancestors lay.

Since the arrival of the ox, people began to think once more about that tree. The elderly people of the kampung told stories about it. In the past, an ox had been tethered to the tree. Some of the people in our neighbourhood believed that the ox had been left by a saint. The ox and the tree were a sacred part of the community's life. No one dared disturb them. Then one day the ox disappeared. No one knew where the ox had gone. All that remained was the tree, the very same tree that stands here now.

The city grew quickly following the disappearance of the ox. People were evicted from their homes, which were then razed. Fires broke out throughout the city. New buildings and new housing complexes were built. Electricity created a new way of life. Communication satellites clustered like stars in the galaxy.

One day, I took a taxi from Glodok in the north to Ciledug in the south. We took the backstreets in order to avoid the congestion between Harmoni and Sudirman. "Kampung life has changed," said the taxi driver. "There are no more respected leaders. Money is the only thing revered." Famous parts of Jakarta such as Sentiong Poncol, Tanah Tinggi, Tanah Sereal, Roxi, Jelambar and Mataram had been replaced by new suburbs: Bintaro, Pondok Indah, Cinere Permai, Lippo City and wherever else there were comfortable apartment blocks. Elevated highways clouded the city's skyline.

The air conditioning in the taxi was getting colder. The driver was chuckling and telling stories. I saw a man perched atop a multi-storey building. "Fire!" he shouted, before quickly covering his mouth.

The traffic was becoming increasingly dense. Kampungs suffered from flooding. Not just floods composed of rainwater, but of people who came from the villages looking for work in factories. They rented houses in our kampung. Soon they outnumbered the original residents. Different customs and languages filled our kampung. Diversity emerged, unity was lost. We were the "emergency entrance" for those who came to the city with nothing.

It felt as though much had been lost. Relationships with the religious and kampung leaders became increasingly bureaucratic. In the past, it'd been like talking with our own parents. Residents were asked to pay all sorts of fees for who knows what. The religious leader at the local mosque was always asking for donations. He had three wives. Residents didn't dare discuss how the money was used: the decisions had already been made by the neighbourhood hierarchy. This same hierarchy was taking more and more payments from the shops that opened up around the kampung.

The kampung was no longer seen as a valid expression of the city. It was known merely as a dirty residential area for the poorest workers and for those who had lost their struggle with the future.

The residents forgot all about the ox. Until one day, when the eldest person in our kampung realised that this ox was the very same ox that had disappeared all those years ago. The news spread quickly. The residents suddenly felt the kampung wasn't simply a place that should be razed or taken over by newcomers. The arrival of the ox reinvigorated our belief in the kampung's significance.

The spirit of the ancestors had to be repatriated to occupy the tree once more. Some of the residents tried to guide the ox back to the tree, but it chose to sleep in front of the prayer house.

The ox had caused something embedded deep within us to rise to the surface. A kind of universe apparent in its gaze and its deep mooing. It had awakened something so powerful within us that one day, I bought a dark blue fridge. My neighbours were a little taken aback by the colour of the fridge, as they were accustomed to fridges being white. It was like they were seeing a new city for the first time when they saw inside the fridge: bright lights

82

and crisp, cold air.

That night, my wife spoke softly while changing our child's diaper. "Our family is now complete with this fridge."

Was it possible that green hills had arisen overnight in our kampung while everyone slept? I could scarcely believe how this fridge could become part of our family, something that could complete the meaning of "family." It was more special than I could ever have imagined. I'd come to believe that life was full of incomprehensible matters. Truly incomprehensible matters.

My newfound wonder abruptly vanished when I heard loud noises coming from my neighbour's house. I heard plates being smashed. In the cacophony I could hear Okot shouting at her husband:

"You're making fun of me! You're so rude to me! You think I've inherited the stupidity of my mother. You treat me like rubbish! You say you're going to leave me. You always insult me! You laugh at me... you think we're so low class we eat rats."[1] Then I heard the door slam and Okot crying.

Not long after, I heard someone knocking at my door. It was Okot. She was still sobbing. She asked if she could stay at our place for a while. And so she did. Our living room was small, but there was enough room for her to sleep there. My wife provided her with a pillow and blanket.

Few knew the details of Okot's life. She was an immigrant from Uganda. Her full name was difficult for us, who were used to short sentences: Okot p'Bitek. She came with her husband, who had since

[1] Quoted from the Ugandan poet, Okot p'*Bitek's Afrika Yang Resah, Nyanyian Lawino* dan Nyanyian Ocol: translated by Sapardi Djoko Damono, Yuyusun Obor publishers: Jakarta, 1988, pages 1-3.

upped and left her. Then she married one of the men who lived in our kampung. He worked as a foreman.

I woke up in the middle of the night. The air was hot. I saw that Okot was asleep; a sleep for the future. I went outside, where it felt a little cooler. The neighbours felt very close. I walked from one laneway to the next until I arrived at the sacred tree. I saw the ox lying on the ground. It was looking in my direction. Its eyes were like a deep and clear well. Maybe the cool air was also emanating from its eyes. There was a coolness at my back.

I suddenly felt full of desire. I approached the ox. It mooed and sniffed my ear. Its nose was cold. A bell hung from its neck. Something had changed in our kampung, in our city. I kissed its back and we rolled around. I took off my clothes. The ox's gaze was like the spirit of a tree that had been uprooted. I entered a new universe through its bellowing. The sound of the bell brought sudden justice to the other clearings within the kampung. Great expanses of lawless green fields.

After everything was over, I came to and realised that many of my neighbours were surrounding me. I was still hugging the ox. I was still naked. I could hear my wife crying. Okot was holding my child. The neighbours led me away with the ox. They didn't know where or how I should be punished. What kind of punishment would be appropriate? I told them myself: "Let me be drowned in the sea with the ox."

My neighbours led me away. My wife cried. I chose the Kamal Estuary as the place where we

84   THE OX ON THE SEABED

would be drowned. I walked with the ox toward the sea. Dawn would break at any moment. People were lined up on the beach. They shone their torches upon me and the ox. The sharp rays of their torch lights trembled on the sea. The mayor also participated in the event, dressed in his everyday safari suit.

The ox and I waded into the sea. Little by little, we went deeper into the water. I began to think about how the city was governed. I was angry. The government never allowed citizens to propose ideas about how the city should be governed. A handful of people made all the decisions. It was they who would determine the price of land on which residents lived, people who spoke short sentences and could never get involved in such antics.

The local leaders encouraged people to sell their land because they took a cut from the sales. They knew when and by how much the price of land would skyrocket. It was they who planned to inflate the price of land. They got in bed with the banks and the other financial institutions inaccessible to people who only spoke in short sentences.

My body and the ox's body were completely submerged. We began to drown. We had lost our land, the place on which to stand firm. We drifted about with the fish. I saw the roots of that sacred tree that grew in our kampung. Those roots spread endlessly, beyond the limits of my vision. I knew this was our destination.

The handful of dirt I'd scooped up from my kampung remained in my mouth. My body and the ox's body became transparent; as transparent as the water at the bottom of the sea. Aaih... coral grew on our bodies, and fish swam through them. A border-less memory of time. Over there.

Home
Telling
a Story
at
460 Watts

Almost two weeks now my shadow has been busy
with our newly rented home. There's almost no
time to relax. Repairing the holey gutters, digging a
hole for water absorption, making a bamboo fence,
painting the bathroom, repairing the door hinges
and windows, installing power cables.

But there's only 460 watts of electricity in this
house. That's not enough for me to live. I've grown
accustomed to living with at least 900 watts of electricity. I can't imagine how one lives with 460 watts
of power. But I'm going to try it, living with 460
watts. Maybe my right hand doesn't need electricity.
I'll try with just my left hand plugged in; my right
hand is more accustomed to working under its own
strength. It can do without electricity.

My bald head always needs a higher dose of
electricity. I get rather irritated with its constant
demands for more. If the power suddenly shorts, I
immediately suspect it's the fault of my bald head,
gluttonous for energy. Sometimes, fuming with re-
sentment, I leave the power off until my head turns
the same greyish colour as the gums of my two dogs.

The money spent on improvements to this house
is beyond reason. Even though I rent it for only ten

million a year. As a writer, I become very flustered. There's no stipend for renting a house. Some friends help me. Ah... Han, Boi, Katon, Wianta... *Tenk u.* Jewe, who I've just gotten to know, fussed about helping with his heavily pregnant wife. *He he, tenk u. Tenk u, man.*

The body of my shadow is like a dark cloud gathering rain. I'm sometimes anxious watching people who work too hard. I worry the rain will spill from my body. And I don't know how to prevent a flood, although I've already made a hole for water absorption as deep as six concrete tubes. Only three meters deep in the front yard. And an open excavation in the backyard.

This home is really a big puddle. The only house that stands about three metres below the highway. The puddle occurred because the soil above the house was leased for coal production. The soil for coal production was taken directly from that leased land. Extracted until there was a big puddle.

Next to the home, there's a simple shack where a farmer usually rests. Sometimes it's like I see the dark shadow of an animal slipping into the shack. Sometimes I'm unsure if that shadow is my shadow jumping from my body to enter that shack alone. But there's never anyone in that shack, only an old bamboo settee for sleeping.

This house has been empty for two years. Nobody rented it. Before, it was inhabited by a group of musicians and artists. They were the types who worked to drive religion, nationality, and the dictatorship of art from their bodies. Let their bodies be free without the dictates of a homemade morality counter to their human nature. I saw them as sufis without a country or religion.

They didn't differentiate between the house and the highway. Their murals filled the house, from the front terrace to the bathroom. Some of the paintings have gone mouldy, a pile of sand fouls the house, and there is an open fire pit made of soil in the middle of the space. The kitchen could be anywhere in that house.

A friend told me that amongst those paintings there is one by a female painter who drove her motorbike home one morning drunk, had an accident and died. That female painter is dead, but her painting is still there. It's in front of me. A painting of a ballet dancer who is trapped on an acrobat's stage.

It's like I'm floating in a winged space. Time becomes a door, but I don't know if it's an entrance or an exit. Maybe they also didn't differentiate between life and death. Maybe their bodies were like wind. Not the same as my shadow, a dark cloud gathering rain.

Our dogs, Kopi and Kremi, mated in this room and Kremi immediately became pregnant. Sometimes they bark at my shadow. If they bark like that, my anxiety reappears. I worry that the black cloud of my shadow will shed rain like a holey sky.

Soft. The wall seems to be exuding sweat not because it's hot, but because it's soft. Glass tiles and old bamboo on the roof. I can see drizzle through those glass tiles, and the occasional flash of lightning. If I watch those glass tiles for almost an hour, I forget whether my body is lying below those glass tiles staring up at them, or whether my body is above and those glass tiles are staring at me.

Between me and the glass tiles are a pair of eyes that live in a box. Those eyes stare at each other. Eyes staring at eyes. Eyes staring at eyes. Eyes staring at eyes. And they cannot lie to each other.

I don't think I want a bathroom. I'll bathe out in the backyard. Others may see me naked, but I see my own body bathing, cleaning myself of filth. This house without a bathroom is like an old legend about an angel who bathes in the river. I don't know whether that angel truly bathes in the river, or if it's really the river that bathes in the body of the angel.

About ten years ago, I visited this house. A house once inhabited by Dadang Christanto, an artist who settled in Australia after the explosion of Reformasi. There were many people who left Jakarta or Indonesia then. Dadang leased this land for fifteen years, and added two small Javanese houses. Ong tells me that Dadang bought these Javanese houses for 650,000 rupiah. That's not enough to live off for a week now.

I feel just how much the value of money is diverging from the value of goods. Money and goods don't provide any measurement of relations between people. Life is lonely like this. A loneliness that makes barbed wire of our necks until the moment we turn on the stove to boil water.

Water boiling in a pan is the same as the fear that roams highways. How unfortunate this life is, if we live only to be constantly confronted by fear.

My shadow begins to install a bamboo fence. Plant wild plants taken from the garden next door. A garden also frightened it will be evicted at any time, to make way for a new building, a house or a shophouse. A home for water or plants is getting harder and harder to find, taken over by concrete.

Then my shadow gets busy dismantling all the concrete covering that yard. Dismantling with an excessive feeling of panic, so the house where we live can share the yard with water. A feeling of panic lest the water tries to sleep with us on the same mattress and pillow. A feeling of panic lest our home turns into a small lake.

"Dang, has this house ever flooded?" I ask Dadang. He was looking for a house in Australia at the same time as I moved into this house. He was moving cities.

"Yeah, if there's a lot of rain, the water will enter from the front yard and the backyard. The yard next door will also send water into the backyard," answered Dadang.

I remembered the thousand statues Dadang installed at Ancol Beach 15 years ago, some drowning in the sea. An installation that reminds me of humans who live in a state of partial drowning. Half their bodies in the water and half out. Humans who, due to particular circumstances, have to live between a fish and a frog. The parts of their bodies in the water can't swim like fish, and the parts of their bodies that are out can't jump like frogs.

I don't know if these statues are now at the

91

bottom of the sea or in a museum overseas. I'm not sure if there is a museum built from the sea, where we can watch crashing waves through the windows of the museum. Dadang's thousand sculptures are inside with the title: "Installation of a Refugee".

The house I live in might also be a museum. A museum for the many stories of its earlier inhabitants. The manager of a furniture store from Jepara. An outcast. When he left this house, he also left some antique furniture that has since disappeared. I was frightened my electric water pump would also be stolen. If someone stole my electric water pump, I'd have to go back to taking water from the well.

This house is certainly telling stories. Almost every day a new theme emerges. And I'm starting to run out of money. I need money so that the house can keep telling stories. Once I've run out of money, this house will be like a coffin. This house is just one step away from being a coffin. If I die, the doors and windows only need to be closed, and the house'll turn into a coffin.

Hmmm…

Hmmm…

He-he-he.

Fitri, my dear, today Petrus will come with Miko. He will come with his bike, its handlebars taller than his head. He will come with a bottle of vodka, a saxophone and a harmonica. He'll sing about post-realism.

My shadow has become rain. Rain that closes in on our bedroom. Water like a great guest arrives from the front yard and the backyard. Water without walls, like a blind creature, enters our home. I greet it with buckets. I keep digging in each spot in the yard that can still be dug to make a seat for the water. I keep digging.

And this house gets deeper and deeper like a well. The time feels cold, it moves from my back to the fingers on my hands that keep hauling away earth with a bucket. My stomach feels like it is bent inwards, holding the weight of the bucket full of soil mixed with water.

I'm very surprised when I suddenly see the shadows of my own eyes reflected by light on the surface of the water in the well. Eyes stare at eyes. I'm confident that it's the shadow of my own eyes, and not the shadow of the eyes of the water. If it's the shadow of the water's eyes, then I have to accept the fact that water has eyes.

The rain begins to end. The sky begins to clear, a thin blue, and colours that are still greyish. Slowly I begin to see the reflection of the pail hanging overhead. The rope made of tyre rubber reaches for the surface of the well. I see life.

Planting Karen in the Middle of the Rain

The VOC came with their weapons, ships, mice, and trading companies. We clashed. Their trade monopoly didn't suit our economic culture. Rain fell without end. Economic conflict became national rebellion. Wind and rain broke dry branches. We could no longer distinguish between trade monopoly and colonialism. Heavy. Their culture was passed down through language, food, clothing, organisations, speeches, and books. Their vile mouths ridiculed me in English.

History moved on. The TV didn't just broadcast weather reports for our cities, but also the cities of the world, the exchange rates of various currencies. Wet season came again. Remember that supermarket? The place where we reorganised so many things, from credit cards to dinner tables. Evictions. National taxes too. A monopoly arranged through customer service. Then the visions of the people progressed on the other end, making the clock tick faster. They think: Globalisation has happened. The world can only be saved through a monopoly. Like an open drain with a hot stench.

All night rain poured. The sky became yet another black chasm. Time limits that boil away.

People reeled beneath them. This is a thought I used to think, when I still believed the sky was full of supernatural occurrences: the traffic of light and the bustle of the spirit world. It became a sort of longing and torture, to assert myself with an unexpected coldness.

Wind brought sheets of rain. Drifting. Slashing at windows. As though there was a fragile world there, in the pounding droplets. Helpless. The only defense was my own body. It made me disbelieve. When flu came in the morning, my body was a puddle of tissue in the toilet. Although I too believe the body is a different universe in the morning. Also a vision of railway tracks. Hard, stiff, and threatening.

That morning, in the middle of the rain, I prepared a shopping list. Coffee. Noodles. Tempeh. Bottled sambal. Watermelon. A tablecloth too. But I was reluctant to buy milk. The advertisements had gotten out of hand. How to fathom: a person dies because they didn't drink milk. My body becomes awful and brittle every time I'm faced with a terror like this. Like the VOC who taunted and teased in arrogantly intoned Malay.

At the door of the supermarket, I took a plastic carry bag. It was getting busy. Old dames and their housemaids. And as usual, I took the opportunity to stare at the shelves laden with fish. My fantasies often conjure up memories as I stand before the frozen fish: Death between blocks of ice. Cold air evaporates. And a bewildering world on a knife's edge.

While selecting a few varieties of instant noodles, I bumped into Karen. She's American. An activist and AIDS counsellor with an NGO. Works in Thailand, a country with many sex workers infected with the HIV virus. The blood of many nations flows in these women's bodies, passed down from their ancestors.

But Karen hates most Indonesian men, who retain a sexual hysteria for foreign women. The history of the VOC is like building many bodies exploded by foreign sensations. Add to this weapons brandished, blonde hair broadcast on TV all day. It seems a lot of personification suffers from this kind of foreignness. Like tomorrow looming in the head-lights of somebody else's car.

Nothing had changed with Karen. Her friend-ly eyes were still protected under a straight fringe. And a sort of independence moving in the patter of her laughter. Often I hope that rain will fall from her fringe, a romance of tropical countries. The romance of a look of sadness and longing inhabit-ing the quivering of bamboo flutes and the beating of the gending. This romance still rules many Asian countries, a sort of inferiority born of the remains of colonialism.

Karen's been in Jakarta for a week. Visiting Halim, her partner. Halim also has a complicated past, born in Serang of Chinese descent. A history of various local cultures and religions deeply entangled within him. He needed another kind of self to unite them all in hatred of arrogant and vacuous power.

We made a plan to watch a film together tomor-row night and went our separate ways. "Why pay for your shopping?" Someone suddenly greeted me, as I queued by the cashier. That person looked like Karen, but they weren't Karen. It was clear from their reproach: they're strange. Estranged from everything.

Their greeting took my fancy, and I immediately left that queue. Went shopping behind "Strange Karen," gliding past the shelves of dried food. She paused to eat a sausage and a raw fish, a cold soft drink in her hand. Then strode through the aisles as though floating, making the supermarket building pulse, leaving the floor like fragments of time evaporating into a black cavern.

"Why do you think this all belongs to them?" She renewed our conversation, pitching raw eggs into the corners of the supermarket. "Take everything you like, we've been extorting ourselves all this time. This is not about morals. This is just a matter of the economy. An arbitrary matter, formalised through economic institutions." Strange Karen then ascended a shelf stacked with biscuits. Sat on top. She threw the empty soft drink can in the direction of the cashier. It sailed through the air and crashed into her forehead. The cashier, beautiful in her blue striped uniform, was killed instantly. Her corpse was taken out immediately and replaced with another cashier.

"The tax you pay on each item of shopping never cared about your tomorrows. We're not required to believe that there is a tomorrow in every bit of cash we possess... Wah!" She then promptly fell asleep on top of the shelves, legs folded beneath her, hair falling loosely down. And once more, there were fragments of time that fell down too.

Her sentences instantly made me a stranger in that supermarket. Without a passport or visa. Between the old dames who purchased cuts of chicken, tomato, cheese, and detergent, hauling them out of their shopping carts. I couldn't feel my breath flow through my neck in this state of strangeness brought on by Karen. As though there was a fridge open in my hands, and someone pulling out the frozen head of a chicken.

"This is by way of introduction..." I said. But suddenly I felt there was nothing but a human in this supermarket, inhabiting my sentences. Strange Karen. An introduction that made me experience things differently, each occurrence around me. Her sentences shook my belief in the persuasiveness of money, tax, laws of trade, even the language I used.

I thought I would exchange my tongue, maybe also exchange my nose for another from a different flu. Wash my brain as required. Change its contents for a different way of thinking. This is a new vulnerability, I thought. A vulnerability that could make me enjoy every change that occured around me, allow me to become anybody at all.

"Let's get out of here," I invited her.

"No. I live here. I'm a creature of the supermarket! I'm used to living here. There's no hard work. The air's fresh. No pollution. I get comfort from the death of frozen fish on these shelves. Like most other people, who live from their own deaths," she said.

I said goodbye to my new companion, Strange Karen. We promised to watch a film together the following night. I left that supermarket, as Karen recommended, without paying for a single item. Strange Karen was right. I walked right past the cashier, gobbling a piece of raw meat as I went, and no one stopped me. Free to blow my nose in the street. I felt I'd entered a new truth. Purer. Stealing without guilt or fear.

I began to think this whole city which I'd known since birth had no past to claim for itself. I took a big standing ashtray from the supermarket patio and threw it into the supermarket. The jangly sound of that rolling ashtray prompted my mind to comprehend another world. A world never offered by goodness or truth. The city is built of the architecture of violence and criminality. My heart once beat in unison with it.

Strange Karen wasn't guilty. Security had no right to manhandle her. Put her in jail just because she stole. Humanity's not as simple as that. I know humanity's got a different love, a different sadness too. Like that black cavern in the sky. Humanity is never guilty. Guilt is just confusion that opens a door for other people in the night. I began cutting slices of sausage on the table. Their red colour tempted me, like lust emerging from a man's deep voice.

Karen, anything could happen in this "Indonesia, hello, hello, Bandung". I'd never heard of Eddy Tansil before. But suddenly he was arrested, involved in billions of dollars of bad loans. Became a magnet for bad press. I didn't know Oki, who killed at the same time as he showed: How easily the young generation can buy a luxury apartment in the USA, in the midst of silly theories about poverty. Does rain fall in your house too?

This would be part of a luxury biography. A biography of those who also don't know how money is made and circulates to the sound of barking and snarling in this country. An unbelievable biography, how luxury brings change.

I also didn't know Marsinah, Karen. But suddenly she became a symbol of the workers' struggle, through her stingingly painful death. A press thirsty for truth, thirsty for a clean society and government, and trembling with fear too, bringing grim details to light for months. Marsinah is dead. And now she's a poster. A slogan. For the suffering and struggle of the workers. The press are the pale ghouls of daybreak.

Many things are born and grow around me. It's not clear who their progenitors are. This is a city without mothers and fathers, I thought. Every inhabitant orphaned by the changes occurring around them.

In the end I didn't see a film with Karen, or her partner Halim. I watched the film with Strange Karen. At the cinema canteen we ordered cold drinks. And a bag of popcorn exploding behind the display window as we watched, like buying the freedom and arrogance of America.

As usual, we didn't need to pay. Entered the projection room without tickets. I bumped into Karen. And the other NGO activists. They didn't only deal with AIDS. Also family planning, rural workforce training, and Third World women's problems. They worked in Thailand, Lombok, and Medan. Meanwhile Halim displayed his serious forehead, and his laughter which kept his body far above the bodies of others.

We watched *In the Name of the Father*. This time Strange Karen didn't talk much, silent within the darkness of the cinema. When Emma Thompson, who played a lawyer in the film, unleashed a barrage of accusations against the British police officers, blunting the British courts' efforts to overcome the IRA's terrorism, Strange Karen suddenly stood up. Her face was like VOC ships burning in the night, juicy watermelon in her eyes.

That night I went home, without Karen, without a country, without a language, without a nationality either. There was no proof of identity whatsoever in my trouser pockets that could explain all this. I knew there was no country in a person's silence. But in the street, I saw Strange Karen alone, under the late night drizzle. She was picking her nose at the bus stop. The street lights weren't bright enough to light her up. Like the weight of the street lights illuminating the city but bringing it no closer to recognising itself.

At home, I found Strange Karen slicing a sausage. Beside her was a cup of coffee, and a cigarette perched on an ashtray. As though beset by sadness all night. An unexpected hesitation. "I've done a lot of things to make myself believe I'm living," she said. Her hair was red and dry, like an unresolved mound of the past. "I've stolen, worn the clothes of many different people. But I don't know how history arrives at night...auh!"

"There's a reality that terrorises me – many

people have died tonight. Many bodies have lost their biographies. Everyone seems to live only for the sake of accompanying themselves. The crisis of relating continues at every counter where we're supposed to pay. This is a sadness unrecognised by God. Now I know why people need deodorant, for the rotten smell of their own bodies losing biographies," she said.

"This soap is for you," I said, hardly believing the sentences I wanted to say. She was silent. Damned for every disbelief. The house was night. Strange Karen was becoming more and more night too. On the slices of sausage, I encountered people's failure to compose their own tomorrows.

Rain fell again. Met each person not brave enough to open the door alone. Then I saw Strange Karen close the fingers of her hand around a knife, and the remaining sausage slices.

The next morning, the supermarket was full of plastic flowers. Bright yellow, with strains of music between the smell of mango and camphor. Air like shaky floating steps. I saw Strange Karen still sleeping on the refrigerator packed with fresh fish, her face preserving a halo of sleep. I chose a few sausages. A few friends were coming over in the afternoon, and a few other Strange Karens. I thought a few slices of sausage would be enough for them. For all the changes they dream of. The dreams of NGO activists in the world of praxis they're so convinced of.

As Strange Karen knew, many dreams only ever change with fairytales, instant noodles, and tissues.

She once changed herself for all of that. And planted herself in the middle of the rain. Like watching the past freeze in your scar tissue. A scar that feels more and more strange, as the rain darkens the window panes. And no one can erase it.

The Toppling of the Letter "f"

I'm a camera left by its owner at the mouth of a rubber plantation. This is my state of existence, which I'll tell you about. As a camera used to being taken here and there, I'm quite accustomed to taking journeys, recording what's considered important, what's hidden. I know how to move fast in particular conditions, shake up important events, or even commit suicide. There's nothing particularly special about me, except that my batteries are flat.

Don't forget, "I'm-on-ly-a-ca-me-ra." In Poyang's house, in kampung Panaragan, I was woken by the sound of a rooster crowing. Rays of morning sun filled the front room of the stilt house, old wood still labouring to support it. My thoughts were like coconut fibre, the discarded carcass of a palm that has been harvested, occupied with the story told by Poyang over the course of a night. A story that feels as though it's coming entirely from a brain on fire. My insides must be unraveled one-by-one to rearrange the fragments of Poyang's story full of political drama: the way of life of a man whose days had been formed by the hot Lampung sun, the politics of the rise and fall of the price of rubber, palm oil, the areca nut, sugar cane, and plantation land conflict. The figure of a tall man, almost always in a hurry, frantically undertaking something. He would wrestle with his destination as he made his way towards it. His laugh was like stone fragments scattered on the road.

Their old house was filled with three generations of photos, tables, cupboards, plates, antique glasses, the cables of indicator lights, lace curtains, chairs, plastic flowers, an ashtray, a tray for drinks served in plastic cups, decorated in a frenzied manner. It all made it pretty hard for someone to move in that guest room. Old stories press a button, take me back in time, help conjure the traffic of voices, the atmosphere, the smell of that guest room.

All of this sounds strange, hurried, pretty hectic, everything that suddenly happened, as Tulang Bawang Barat (Tubaba) was confirmed as the newest administrative district of Lampung Province. The residents were as though born again, looking at the sun as if they owned it. Suddenly everything became important, sacred tombs, statues of crocodiles, stilt homes, old musical instruments, cannons, spears, Lampung tapestries, recipes, important figures long forgotten, names of the past, the traditional ceremonial throne of the Pepadun people, a statue of the head of a buffalo, traditional shirts, plants, fish in the river... But suddenly the price of rubber fell. Future sorcery vibrated in the stillness of the rubber plantations.

I could feel all of this pulsing like a wave that shifts time again. Politics, the economy, pulsed with the same importance as culture.

THE TOPPLING OF THE LETTER "F"

"What's this?" I wondered.

"A wave of history that has suddenly awoken after a long time in the grave." I recoiled. Angry. Not trusting myself. My lens panicked, zooming in and out with jerky movements. The macro lens that had chased the details of the hidden knitting behind the golden thread of a Lampung tapestry. Searched for itself in many tight corners, dazzled by the flash between the histories of Lampung, Banten, Palembang, Sriwijaya... An index of the ethnicities that writhe in search of form between a scarcity of artefacts, blurring and commingling with narratives of the arrival of Islam.

Perhaps there would be no record of all this if Reynier de Klerck, a VOC diplomat, hadn't come and resolved the conflict between the Palembang and Banten sultanates, creating Menggala (the meeting point of the Way Kanan and the Way Kiri rivers and the centre of their feud, around the time the Dutch East Indies fell into the hands of the English at the beginning of the 18th century). Or the arrival of Captain Jackson, Raffles' emissary sent to inventorise the Palembang sultanate for the powers supplying pepper to the global market. Both of them made important notes as they advanced their political and military agendas.

Most of what they recorded, important sites of human habitation, were probably buried in the Krakatoa eruption of 1883. Old sites of Sumatra that held an archive on the mutual permeation of Animism, Hinduism, Islam, Europe commingling with the sediment and dust of the Krakatoa eruption.

"We want a TV station, radio, a newspaper press, books, a theatre, gallery, museum, recording studio, library, public park, playground, laboratory"… the voices that will soon clamour to move the floor of history they are building.

Faint conversation in the Lampung language emerges from the bathroom located beside my room. A mother washes her child who is about to go to school. Bursts of the Lampung language are interspersed with the sound of water from a plastic scoop being poured over the child's body. The sound of water and the sound of language take turns making a new space for listening. I suspect that the morning bustle has also begun in the kitchen. Conversation in the Lampung language mingling with spices and firewood.

They're proud to feel they have ancestors, because they have the Kaganga script that is said to derive from the same source as the Rencong script, Rejang Bengkulu, Sunda, Lontara with Pallawa hues. I don't know what storm of history drowned these scripts, replacing them with the Latin script that I use to write this story. The fall of a script means the fall of the civilisation and culture of the users of that script. At least that's what I once heard said by a theorist on the relationship between language and culture. Those who believe that language is the first technology humankind used to process their cultural images. "Death to language!" Sometimes I challenge myself to commit suicide via language.

Jural, Poyang's friend who works as a firefighter

in Tubaba, woke us with a sound like the limb of a rubber tree that has just been punctured to allow sap to ooze out. He brought nasi uduk for breakfast. Tea and coffee in small glasses was assembled on the guest table in the front yard. A sofa with torn upholstery also delivered a story about the rise and fall of the price of rubber, the backbone of the family economy in Tubaba.

I felt reluctant to wake up. In my mind, a figure was emerging. I didn't recognise the figure. Had this figure materialised out of the stories I'd heard last night, or had she come to create me so that I could be "someone who is here" in kampung Panaragan? A kampung that, approaching afternoon, was almost completely fenced in by the sun. That figure forced me to stay asleep today. Slept all day in the room so as to enjoy her presence.

"Who are you?" I asked.

"I don't know," she answered. "Does it matter?"

"Why?" I asked.

"Humanity uses too many names," she replied.

"Why are you following me?" I asked the figure again. She was making a big impression on me.

"Ask yourself."

I finally awoke once I had a name for this figure. Her name was Sindi Kaganga. A young woman almost 23 years of age. Her first name was an old Lampung name hardly ever used anymore. Her surname used the name of the script of Lampung. It wasn't an easy name for me, who knew nothing about Lampung. But the biggest problem was: this figure was a young woman. A male writer like my-

THE TOPPLING OF THE LETTER "F"

self can't easily convince the reader that this figure with such an important name was a woman.

"Sindi Kaganga is your name?" I asked.

"Yeah," she answered.

She was a woman with a face like most Straits Chinese people. A face not too different from Stanislaus Yangni, a woman from Lampung who now works as a historian in Yogyakarta. Also not too different from the eyes of Jurai who had just brought us nasi uduk for breakfast. Sindi's hair was longer, darker, thicker. Hair that appeared to be cared for using natural coconut milk grown in Tubaba.

I awoke. Sindi soon vanished, returned to life outside of script. I made the bed. Turned off the fan while holding back the urge to pee. When I opened the door to the room and looked towards the front yard, I encountered a neat grave by my feet. A grave with a wall surrounding it, and a zinc roof. Previously I'd thought this grave was a goat pen. I hadn't recognised it, because we'd arrived at Poyang's family home at twilight. The grave of someone considered sacred. They had long hair that no pair of scissors could cut. The family of the deceased had moved somewhere else. Nobody took care of the grave anymore.

The sun was getting hotter as we left the kampung and approached the regent's official residence. Passing old stilt homes. At first glance, all the houses looked the same. But gradually the differences between the architecture of Lampung, Palembang and Pagaruyung were discernible from their various styles of engravings. The differences were more

THE TOPPLING OF THE LETTER "F"

noticeable again when we entered kampung Bandar Dewa. A clean kampung. I was impressed that it still functioned as a Lampung cultural site. Some houses had started to change all of that, their walls painted in multi-colours. Satellite dishes and cars appeared on the roofs and in the yards of several homes, the fruits of the rubber harvest when the price of rubber was still high.

The official residence of the regent stood like the regal building of the VOC governor, white walls and columns looming large. This building with its strange appearance stood in the centre of Tubaba, the architecture of which otherwise consisted of stilt houses, whose contours were much more representative of the contours of the rubber and palm oil plantations distinctive of Tubaba. Two rivers (Way Kanan and Way Kiri) majestically criss-crossed the regency like a pair of ancient dragons. The colour of chocolate writhed on the surface of the rivers, giving never ending life to the inhabitants. Several species of birds often crossed over them. Fishermen occasionally passed in slim wooden boats. When the wet season began, the bodies of the rivers would expand, submerging the banks they inhabited during the dry season.

The regent (Mr Umar) greeted us wearing only a t-shirt and shorts. His gaze was full, controlling the space around it. A regent who was still young, tall, held himself as equal to others. He had no interest in elevating himself as a regent in the sense of "a ruler". Today, Hanafi and Hendro Rukmono, painters from Jakarta, would give a drawing workshop for the schoolchildren of Tubaba. Their teachers would also join the workshop.

"The day is really hot," Sindi was suddenly beside me.

"Where are you from?" I asked.

"Panaragan," she answered. "But now I'm in Semarang. Taking archaeology".

"What can you use from here for your study?" I asked. "Will you study the river as archaeology?"

"No," she replied.

"Stories," she said. "Stories, fairy tales, will be my archaeological field."

"Digging them up…"

"With a saw and a bulldozer…." Sindi continued.

"We treat stories like debris buried in layers of earth for thousands of years," I continued the conversation.

"You still trust language enough to use the expression thousands of years? What do you imagine with these thousands of years you speak of? Your body and language immediately cease to be able to explain it," Sindi set my brain on fire.

"Archaeology is full of catastrophe," I thought.

"Don't forget that there was the Krakatoa eruption here. We don't know how many times that terrific mountain has vomited up its guts, burying Lampung," continued Sindi. "We're only familiar with Krakatoa, 1883. This is because of the notes of a Dutch businessman in the sugar trade, Johannes Beijerinck, and a geologist, Rogier Verbeek. Have you ever seen the film 'Krakatoa, East of Java', made by Sam Miller in 2006?" she asked. I shook my head.

"Watch it. You can find it on YouTube," she continued. "I really want to be able to read the poem, Lampung Karam, written by an author of that time, Muhammad Saleh. You can imagine his ingenuity: a country ridden with water and ash. You can picture water and ash riding a horse. The horse is Lampung. Who hasn't ridden Lampung?" Sindi chattered away, as though she'd known me for a long time.

"Have you ever ridden a horse? There should be lots of horses here, if it weren't for those hellish motorcycles offered on credit for a speed that's unnecessary here," she kept on.

"Death to the word 'should', and the dictionary can be the coffin," I thought. I'm truly perturbed each time I hear the word 'should'. Suddenly I'd been invaded by archives and problems brought by Sindi. I suspected Sindi had already turned herself into a warehouse of lonely archives. At the tallest peak of the hills surrounding the hamlet of Kepayang, the village of Kelawi, Bakauheni, I knew research had been conducted into a boat believed to have been shipwrecked there when Krakatoa erupted.

"An archive? To hell with archives. My brain is on fire." I began to feel in disarray. I walked into the backyard of the regent's home. A forest of young rubber trees stretched out before me. My lungs took in the rich oxygen produced by the trees. Trees known for their capacity to absorb carbon dioxide. An old woman with her whole body wrapped in cloth was tapping the sap of the rubber trees. Her hands and feet moved from one tree to another.

From afar, the woman seemed to be tapping

silence. A silence that seemed far more real than my presence here. I inhaled that permeating silence. Stepping softly, it held my hand, but I couldn't feel it. A silence that became myself. I was no longer a script. But not for long. Sindi arrived, hovering over the rubber trees. She was like a breeze that blows, then pools beneath the trees' leafy exuberance. I took it all in as though watching an animation. The glow of the sun passed through each gap in the leaves and onto the branches, or infiltrated the dried leaves making up the tender floor of the forest. Rustling as I stepped on rubber seeds. Sindi's body suddenly ricocheted like a rubber ball and crashed before me.

"Rubber once changed the world," she said.

Sindi really was an archive. I had no interest in archives. Oxygen, rubber forests, and silence were more my thing. "Long ago, an Aztec from Mesopotamia made the first ball out of latex, the sap of the rubber tree. Your generation can also make balls from latex, no? Latex is spread out in a vast field, allowed to dry, then it's rolled to become a ball with that typical latex smell."

Sindi began to think she knew more than I did.

"Get this archive away from my silence," I thought.

"The rubber balls they made bounced beautifully. Bernal Diaz del Castillo, a Conquistador, believed the spirit of Satan resided in those rubber balls," Sindi continued.

"You're Satan. Archives are Satan," I thought. The figure of Sindi began to blur, vanished, turned into rubber tree seeds before me. I picked up the seeds and put them in my bag. Perhaps the drawing workshop would be finished by now. I returned to the workshop, but the activities were still underway. I approached a teacher who was assisting his students to draw a tiger in all of the primary colours. The children drew as though they were using house paint. The tiger vibrated and seethed with melting colours.

The drawing teacher, a young man whose appearance was more like that of a construction worker, began to speak in a language that wasn't clear to me. I was startled by the language he used. I imagined that this teacher spoke in a language he'd invented just for his students. Hanafi approached and told me this teacher was deaf. I was surprised and amazed at the same time. That a deaf teacher worked as a drawing instructor at this school. Extraordinary. I imagined a blind person teaching fine arts, a deaf person teaching music, and a mute teaching poetry.

I approached the vice-regent, Mr Fauzi. His face, approaching old age, appeared melancholy. I stared at the schoolchildren learning to draw.

"Look at those handsome schoolchildren, those beautiful girls, so clever... once they graduate, they'll leave Tubaba. Continue their schooling outside. And won't return. They'll find a family and work outside..." he said sadly as though to himself.

I was moved by his words. What could be done? Education had made thousands of villages lose their best generation. Why must universities be founded in the city and not in the village? The fire in my brain began to flicker again.

As evening approached, a kampung masseuse massaged me in the house offered to guests of the regent, one of the buildings on the property of the official residence. Mr Umar (the regent of Tubaba) lay on the carpet and chatted with some friends not far from the spot where I was being massaged. It was a strange event for me, being massaged with a regent beside me. Something happened, grew and changed. I hope it's water to extinguish whichever brain is being set on fire this time. The drifting smell of the sugar factory, an important industry since the colonial period, filled my brain. An industry that will come out to play when the elections for the district head begin to heat things up in whatever region of Lampung.

In the morning as I readied myself to leave Tubaba, I ate nasi uduk with Sindi at the Panaragan market. "Do you have a book on the history of Lampung?" I asked a female bookseller at one of the stalls. I was startled to see a book stall in the middle of this market. A market that mostly sold groceries and other household items. Listening to the women gossip, making up naughty phrases they couldn't possibly utter when they were at home. Several among them were even bold enough to flirt with men. Although most of them wore hijabs. A market that suddenly displayed cosmopolitan colours, distinct from the ordinary faces we'd seen when we entered the kampungs of Tubaba.

"Don't have one, sir." replied the bookseller. I

looked at the books for sale. Not many. All of them were religious books. The Lampung language, Javanese, Balinese and even the Minang dialect, mixed with the smell of fish and the sound of a coconut grating machine. An empty market was an important indication of whether the price of rubber was rising or falling. The fall of the price of oil on the global market, the decline of industry in China, the emergence of Vietnam and India as new suppliers on the global rubber market after Indonesia, Thailand and Malaysia, were new factors in the price of rubber. Farmers had to quickly switch to another plant whose price was rising, like the areca nut, or sugar cane whose market demand was steady.

After wandering around the market with Sindi eating nasi uduk with omelet, tempeh and sambal, I returned to that book stall and asked again, just to make sure:

"Do you have a book on the history of Lampung?"

The woman guarding that book stall was wary, stared at me as though I was the resident thug of the market showing himself for the first time. I went to the store opposite the book stall, bought an old iron that still used coal for 90,000 rupiah, and a traditional Lampung bridesmaid doll for 20,000 rupiah. I displayed these two items to the bookseller, as though I'd succeeded in buying a book on the history of Lampung made of an old coal-powered iron and a Lampung bridesmaid doll. This appeared to confirm to the woman that I was the new resident thug of the market. A thug searching for "a book on the history of Lampung".

Almost four hours of travel brought me to the port of Lampung. I continued my journey in an old bus that had long been famous for making the journey across Sumatra. I entered the bus as though entering a rickety history. Four hours later the bus had traversed a winding road, passed hills that sheltered it from the hot sun, rows of shop houses, factory buildings, and arrived at the port of Bakauheni as late afternoon set in. By then, Sindi Kaganga was no longer by my side. She'd vanished, living outside of script.

I took in the sea, the hills in the distance, the breeze, the expanse of sky and horde of clouds constantly changing, coffee, pop-mie instant noodles and jamu for men, a traditional herbal medicine, while chatting with a group of gold miners from Bukit Tinggi, Tasik and Garut, or young adults from Sibolga who were going to Jakarta to seek their fortunes. A portrait here and there while fantasising... As if I was living in the year 1883, right on August 26 when Krakatoa erupted... The walls of the mountain that tumbled, a 40 metre-high wave that rose in a storm of tsunamis, a succession of waves that hunted down everything on land, a hot cloud that hit tall hills... Millions of cubic metres of material from the mountain that darkened the sky.

I arrived in Depok at 11pm.

Sindi Kaganga awoke tossing and turning in the room of her boarding house in kampung Bustaman, Semarang. She had just received a call from her father in Tubaba. The price of rubber had fallen. He couldn't afford to pay for her education anymore.

She would have to return to Panaragan, leave the archaeology classes behind. As a young woman, she was helpless to refuse her father's wishes, although she tried to convince him that she'd look for the money herself in order to continue her schooling. It was still too early to accept these abrupt changes. To drop out of university just because of the price of rubber.

"Rubber really is the spirit of Satan," thought Sindi. Agreed with that Conquistador from Spain, who believed the Aztecs from Mesoamerica had stored the spirit of Satan in the balls they made out of rubber.

Sindi used the rest of the money sent by her parents to buy a ticket back to Lampung. There was no money left to buy gifts for her little sister who'd requested a traditional Semarang striped shirt fashionable in the city. In the Lampung airport, the hot sun greeted Sindi together with her parents. Her mother brought her a Lampung tapestry woven with golden thread.

For her, the tapestry of Lampung was poetry. There was a narrative stored within its texture that was no longer recognised by her generation. The woven motifs contained a certain conception of their spirits. A narrative not too different from the tapestries of other parts of the archipelago, or in particular motifs on Javanese cloth that contain prayers.

"You have to wear this now," said her mum, handing over the tapestry.

The poetry she saw in that tapestry soon vanished. Sindi opened the fabric only to find it was a hijab. Unconsciously, she stroked her long black hair. Hair that grew thick, cared for with coconut cream from her kampung in Panaragan.

"Why, ma?" asked Sindi.

"All the women in the kampung wear one now," her mother answered.

"Sorry Ma... sorry... this hair, the gift of God, is far more beautiful than that fabric made in a factory, ma..." replied Sindi while stroking her hair.

Sindi appeared confused. Her mother was also confused. Neither of them understood what had happened. Where could their perspectives possibly meet, after Sindi had politely refused her mother's gift?

Sindi looked away, leaving her parents while pulling her suitcase behind her. Her mother intimately understood her child's train of thought, not easily bent into something she didn't yet comprehend. Her child was already familiar with airplanes, using the sky as their highway. While she herself had never left Tubaba, only occasionally having visited Lampung city to go shopping when the price of rubber was high, twenty thousand rupiah per kilo. Now the price was only seven thousand rupiah per kilo. She'd never even ridden a ferry across the Sunda Strait, famous for Krakatoa.

Sindi's mother was aware that she and her child belonged to different generations. How should she orient herself towards her daughter who'd already become the child of another civilisation? She gazed at the figure of her child. Her face resembled that of a Straits Chinese, her father's lineage, with her slender woman's figure and the bold contours of her bones.

It was early afternoon as they entered Tubaba. The area was now a regency of Lampung. Several new streets had been built. Some new statues stood, including a statue of a dragon mythologising the origins of the Lampung people. Sindi suddenly felt a hunger to absorb all of the changes that had occurred in the area. She couldn't be rushed into accepting the new government's efforts to present the area as an icon of Lampung. She was hesitant to accept a vision that territorialised identity. For her, Lampung was a cosmopolitan society still seeking after its form, an area of heavy traffic at the crossing point between Java and Sumatra. At this stage, Sindi could see a trajectory that could perhaps indeed be taken by Tubaba, a thought through which she began to understand the existence of the white statue of the dragon. The statue of Rato Nago Besanding, which until now she'd only seen as a photo on the internet.

Rubber plantations, palm oil, sugarcane, returned to Sindi's memory, hills and the sheen of freshly asphalted streets. She felt a little surprised, couldn't find the pulse of life inflected by plantation culture there. Many people passed in cars. As though they were all residents of elsewhere, rushing by at high speeds. Everything she saw appeared only as a scene from the hilly and forested highways.

"Your friends, Siti, Ranau, Hara... they've all married and had children," her mother invited Sindi to speak, trying to overcome the feeling of foreignness that had ambushed the relationship between mother and child.

"Everybody has to marry in the end, mama," replied Sindi soberly, not knowing how to take her mother's provocation. "Who is Hara's husband, ma?" Sindi tried to ease the conversation in another direction.

"Isbedi…"

Sindi tried to remember Isbedi, a friend from high school. He had become a well-known poet and journalist. Her thoughts floated to the world of relations between men and women. Relations that were in fact simple, but became complicated because of the silly matter of matrimony. Matrimony ridden with values whose connection with matrimony itself was unclear. Made into an institution to preserve those values. Sometimes Sindi wanted to know whether her mother was happy living with the husband who happened to be Sindi's father. But she'd never been brave enough to ask. It would only tear open a wound that had been closed with responsibilities and household routines. A question that set Sindi's brain alight.

Sindi was amazed to see three girls walking home from school. The presence of those three girls walking home made all of the scenery around her appear fabulous. The link between humans and nature. Reminding her of the farmers of Java who for the most part still carried their animal feed on their heads, or by a bicycle moving at a pace that could be followed by the naked eye.

Sindi's heart beat faster as the vehicle carrying

THE TOPPLING OF THE LETTER "F"

her entered kampung Panaragan. She saw people gathered in the village hall, conducting an auction of fish caught by local fishermen in rivers and ponds. Auctions that had become special events in riverside kampungs. The starting prices were announced, the auctioneer blurting out the economic mantra of riverside societies.

In the front yard of her childhood home, Sindi caught a glimpse of her uncle, Si Bugu, sweeping. She dearly missed this mute uncle of hers. Sindi immediately ran to hug him. This simple uncle of hers became jittery upon receiving her hug. He saw that his niece had become a grown woman. As a mute man without family, he trembled feeling the hug of this niece whose body was now that of a young woman.

The evening was the most extraordinary time on the day of Sindi's arrival. Dinner made Sindi enjoy her mother's cooking again.

"Wow seruit!" Sindi squealed upon seeing seruit, a traditional dish of Pepadun.

"Thank you, ma," Sindi soon smelt the delicious smell of the Chitala fish grilled with shrimp, mangoes, garlic, turmeric, ginger, soy sauce, and sambal, ambushing her senses. Seeing that dish spread over the dinner table, including salted egg seasoned with shrimp, Sindi immediately forgot her studies, abruptly brought to an end by a fall in the price of rubber. She realised food was an identity immediately experienced through smell and the tongue enjoying that food. It was that seruit dish that made Sindi feel she'd come home.

THE TOPPLING OF THE LETTER "F"

As dinner unfolded, Sindi occasionally caught the gaze of her uncle, Si Bugu, fixed on a certain part of her body. She knew that gaze was no longer the gaze of an uncle, but the gaze of a man.

Whatever had happened to Si Bugu while she attended university in Semarang, Sindi still saw her uncle as a unique man. Firstly, because his name was Si Bugu, precisely the same name as an important figure within Lampung literature. Secondly, his character was similar to that figure within Lampung literature: stupid. But he had an unexpected intelligence that only functioned when it was truly needed. Sindi didn't know why her uncle had been given the name of that literary figure from Lampung. The only difference was that her uncle was mute.

For Sindi, her uncle embodied a metaphor for oral literature that had fallen silent. A theme that often tempted her to use archaeological methods to re-read the ciphers of oral literature as a script. But her studies had ended because of a fall in the price of rubber. At the same time, she found herself again in contact with her uncle, Si Bugu. This encounter created a new agenda for her, because of the unexpected turn her life had taken. She didn't know what would happen next.

In Lampung literature, Si Bugu is narrated as the obedient child who does whatever is asked of him by his mother. His mother once said to him, if you propose to a woman, and that woman remains silent, it means she's accepted your proposal. One day, Si Bugu saw a woman reclining in a rubber plantation. Si Bugu approached that woman and proposed to her. The woman remained silent. Then the mother saw Si Bugu returning home carrying the body of a woman who would be her daughter in law. Si Bugu said that his wife was asleep, so his mother told him to lay her down in the guest room.

The next morning the mother smelt a bad odour coming from the room where the woman slept. The woman who Si Bugu had carried home was in fact a corpse. The woman was silent when Si Bugu proposed to her because she was already a corpse when he saw her sprawled in the rubber forest. Everything that smells rotten is a corpse that must be buried, said his mother. One day his mother farted, emitting a smell similar to that of the decomposing corpse. Si Bugu then tried to bury his mother. She fled. That's Si Bugu, that's how he thinks. But after all that he still manages to become a king with a dutiful queen by his side.

That night Sindi slept restlessly. She was visited by many memories from her past. Some photos were still pasted to the wall, her school bag, shoes, a blanket, watch, sandals, towel, mirror, wardrobe... 150 tigers suddenly descending thunderously upon the river from the forest. The sound of their roaring, their leaps as they ran, made the ground vibrate. The roar of 150 tigers as though emitting a thousand-watt wave of electricity with high voltage. Everything suddenly vibrated.

Sindi was perplexed to find herself in a dream world with 150 tigers. She awoke with hunted breath. A dream that'd made her enter an episode from William Marsden's book about the history of Sumatra. Sindi stopped reading that book right at the section about Sumatran tigers. Sumatrans believe their ancestors are tigers. Owing to this, some of them are still afraid to mention the word tiger, and instead say the word "ancestor". They also use the word "ancestor" for crocodiles. One myth came from the forest, the other from the river.

Where have all those rare animals gone? Have we hunted down and slaughtered all of our ancestors? Murdered the myth created by our ancestors who preceded us by hundreds of years.

"Death to archives," thought Sindi in order to return to her sleep and extinguish the thunderous dream of 150 tigers. A dream that'd made her feel she was being sucked into the vortex of the past. An archaic dream. Archaic restlessness. Throwing her headlong into the past, just as that area had become a new regency with a bright future. A politics of governance that made the indexes of ethnicity writhe as they were transformed into new technologies. Sindi knew at that moment that this archaic body would soon tremble. All the while her mother was asking her to wear a hijab.

Sindi patiently attempted to sleep so she could soon visit the Panaragan market. Go shopping for household items with uncle Bugu. At the market, Sindi and Bugu ate nasi uduk with gusto. The market was quiet. Several stalls didn't appear to be selling. Sindi spoke with some sellers who remembered her. Finally, almost all of the stallholders greeted Sindi. She wasn't prepared to negotiate these communal relations. She hadn't been so conscious of them when she was younger. A form of relating that was still alive and well at this market. She felt that Semarang, where supermarkets and malls were omnipresent, had lost some of its character. She didn't know how much had been lost. Or perhaps it was Tubaba that had changed completely, except for this market.

"Do you have a book on the history of Lampung?" Sindi asked the bookseller. The woman keeping the shop stared at Sindi fixedly.

"No," replied the seller, staring at Sindi, thinking of the male customer and now this woman who was looking for the same book: a history of Lampung.

"What good is a history book, compared to a book on religion?" thought the bookseller. Sindi looked at the books for sale. Not many. They were all on religion.

Then Sindi went to the shop opposite the book stall, purchased an old iron that still used coal, and the doll of a traditional Lampung bridesmaid. Sindi didn't know why she'd purchased these two items, even though there was already an electric iron at home. She displayed these two items before the bookseller, as though she'd succeeded in buying a book on the history of Lampung made out of an old coal-powered iron and the doll of a Lampung bridesmaid. Sindi was pleased with that vision. Uncle Bugu was astonished by the conduct of his niece. His tongue wanted to leap, overcome his disability and immediately talk with this niece who amazed him.

In the rubber plantation, Sindi returned to tap the rubber trees for sap with her uncle Bugu. She was a little nervous as she gripped the handle of the sharp sickle used to carve into the trunk of the rubber trees to make the sap flow. Half a coconut shell was bound below the wound. That knife scared her. Sindi continued tapping the trees, forgetting the fear that had suddenly assaulted her. The figure of her uncle Bugu was no longer visible, consumed by the glimmer of light passing through the branches above. Her lungs took in the oxygen emitted by the rubber trees.

Sindi began to submit to the ageless silence of the plantation. A silence that felt much more real than her presence there. A silence that permeated, inhaled. Stepping softly, it held her hand, but she couldn't feel it. A silence that became herself. Suddenly, she spotted Bugu moving from one tree trunk to another. She saw Bugu pouring out the white liquid in the coconut shells so that the rubber would reach a level of viscosity and a quality ready for sale.

Sindi would wash as soon as she got back to her house, she told herself. Her body was itchy because of the insects biting her in the plantation. Her immunity had vanished after three years away from Tubaba. The insects in the rubber plantation were no longer wary of her body. Sindi felt afraid of the changes facing her.

Her giddy feeling soon vanished, when her mother came and took her home.

"You went to the market today?" her mother

THE TOPPLING OF THE LETTER "F"

asked.

"Yeah," replied Sindi, surprised by her mother's question.

"You also went to the rubber plantation with Uncle Bugu?" her mother continued the line of questioning.

"Yeah," answered Sindi.

"People at the market have started to talk about you. It's only two days you've been here. People in the kampung have also started to talk about you. Only two days."

"Why, ma? Do I have to ask for permission now to go to the market and the rubber plantation?" asked Sindi.

Her mother returned with the fabric she'd brought to the Lampung airport. Sindi looked at the fabric. But didn't take it. Sindi recognised her mother again at that moment. A mother whose way of thinking wasn't so different from her own. When she was with her mother, she sometimes felt she was talking to herself, because her mother's way of thinking wasn't so different from her own. But this time, her mother was taking a position altogether other to her own. She knew what to do. Her mother could suspect what she wanted about Sindi's behaviour. They entered a quarrel from which they could not find common ground.

Her mother then left Sindi in her room. Sindi wanted to cry. If only she had stayed in Semarang, been a different person in the city. But she wasn't a rebel. She was no more interested in becoming a rebel than she was in becoming a political lobbyist. She knew her tears had no use. Everything was already clear.

At the same time, she heard the sound of crying coming from elsewhere. Sindi left her room, following the sound of sobbing. She parted the lace curtains that covered the door to Uncle Bugu's room. In the room, Sindi saw her uncle Bugu crying, facing the direction of the window. It was the first time she'd seen him cry. Below that window, she knew, was the grave of a sacred figure whose hair no scissors in the world could cut.

Did Uncle Bugu have a connection with that sacred person's grave? Did Uncle Bugu hear my quarrel with my mother? Sindi was engrossed by these questions. She entered the room and hugged the body of her uncle whom she dearly loved. His tears sounded melancholic. Sadness overflowing from his body. Sindi gently stroked her uncle's back, kissed him. Kissed the back of a man whose sadness was intangible. Submerged in the language of muteness understood by nobody else throughout his life. An oral literature buried deep within layers of earth that wouldn't be dug up again.

Outside, Sindi saw several residents walking with strained faces. One of them entered the yard and locked the gate to their house. One of them stood guard. One of them departed somewhere with several others. Sindi sensed that something was happening. Her mother pulled her inside, and immediately closed the doors and windows.

"What's happening, ma?" asked Sindi.

"Thugs stirring up a riot…"

Sindi knew thugs didn't only exist in cities, where the governments were, but even in the art world, even in the forest.

"A riot about Cultivated Land, Lot 44," continued her mother.

"Where's dad, ma?" asked Sindi anxiously.

"There's a resident's meeting, but I don't know where your uncle Bugu is."

Sindi was suddenly fearful. She went to the room in search of her uncle, who she'd left only a few minutes before, still in tears. The room was empty. But her mother stopped her from searching any further. Her mother couldn't permit anything happening to Sindi. After only a handful of days in her kampung, Sindi had to face unannounced power outages. Disrupting the work of preparing her university files on her laptop, and breaking the electrical equipment in the house.

Hundreds of residents searched for loved ones who had become victims of the rioting. Four houses and six motorcycles had been burned to the ground. Bugu was somewhere in the midst of this tense atmosphere.

"Hunt them down! Chase them!"

"We must demand revenge!"

"Calm! Calm!"

"Burn it!"

"Control yourself!"

Several voices in several languages mingled in their shouts. Cold and pure thoughts mingled with brains that were on fire. The air was burning with heat emitted from a hot potato controlling the emotions of the masses.

Police and firefighters arrived. They discovered a victim who had been shot dead. How can a firearm enter the eternal silence of the forest? Why was there a catastrophe whose movements couldn't be predicted hidden beneath that silence? The riot wasn't just about the extortion of sharecroppers, renters of farmland, but also the force applied to make farmers sell their harvests to particular sellers at cheap prices.

The market didn't know that the cassava, corn, and rubber cultivated by farmers was more than just cassava, corn, and rubber. It was also unexpected catastrophes, conflict, extortion, murky transactions, victims. Sindi tried to quieten her anxiety by tidying her uncle's bedroom. A room with an iron bed, a kind she hadn't seen since living in Semarang. A wooden-walled room painted blue, a wooden floor that issued a creaking sound when she walked on it. She separated the lace blinds covering the window, and looked again at the grave of the sacred person whose hair couldn't be cut. A mysterious grave that had intrigued her since she was a child. A poster of Rambo and the figure of Sukarno were plastered on the wall of her uncle's room. The poster paper had yellowed. Sindi didn't know what her uncle made of these figures.

As she covered the pillows with a sarong embroidered with flowers, Sindi smelt her uncle's distinctive scent. Her heart beat faster. She remembered that her uncle had once fallen in love with a woman from the kampung involved in the recent rioting.

131

"Could Bugu be there?" Was Bugu really a creation of Lampung oral literature that was now falling silent, only to be reawoken at every whiff of a corpse? Sindi felt her brain set ablaze again by the archaic stories that ruled her. Stories where the relationship between men and women always represented the springboard for achieving spiritual elevation and high social-political standing in society.

"This pillow that still contains the sweat of Uncle Bugu, this is oral literature," thought Sindi. "Orality is not always literacy," Sindi had to accept this point in order to understand all of the archaic turmoil that controlled her instincts, freeing them from her DNA. Unconsciously, After preparing the pillow, Sindi pressed it against her breasts, ruminating on the appearance of archaic instincts and the problems of DNA. She didn't know why she'd done it. She didn't need a troublesome rationale for something natural that moved in a woman's body.

"What's a pillow? Just a place to rest our heads? What are stories? What are catastrophes?"

Sindi left her uncle's room where silence was as though eternally confined. As evening approached, the riot was put down. Sindi didn't understand where a phrase like this had come from: "the riot was put down". But Uncle Bugu and her father hadn't returned home yet. Her anxiety increased dramatically when her father returned home alone around 10 at night, saying Uncle Bugu was nowhere to be seen. The police were searching for him, alongside pursuing the group who'd triggered the riot.

I've returned to the last section I wrote above.

Sometimes I hate myself. What right do I have to write someone else's story? Isn't this an issue of human rights? I'm a thief in the world of narrative, entering the reports of journalists who were on the scene, while I just download them via the internet. Watch the incident through a video report. Enter into the language they're using, where sometimes the word "conflict" is written "conplict". The Lampung dialect which is more comfortable with the letter "p", making the letter "f" powerless.

I want to delete the last section above. But if I delete it, this whole piece of writing will have no meaning whatsoever. An author who can't stop making catastrophic elements the heart of his writings. The world of drama, tragedy, Greek aesthetics, still control the current era.

"Death to tragedy," I think, while imagining the debris of Athens and the collapse of the Greek economy. I only want to communicate that when an author plans to write a tragedy, the author experiences the same anxiety, whether he writes the tragedy or not.

Below the stilt house that is no longer orderly, I sit on a rock, stare at a few scattered things. I see Sindi guide children down the wooden stairs, go to tap the rubber trees with her mother and her little sister. Without Uncle Bugu. I don't know Uncle Bugu's fate after the riot yesterday. Sindi's father is still seeking his whereabouts.

I climb the stairs. The house is empty. Nobody there. Everything I see in the house suddenly appears important, profound. Things that share the silence with one another, share a civilisation that can no longer be touched, mixing with various measurements of time, forming a present that is not alone. I sip the remains of coffee from a glass. It's getting on to afternoon. I leave that stilt house, look for Sindi in the rubber plantation.

I take in the unique oxygen of the rubber plantation, the ageless silence, the contours of the branches. I try to close my eyes so that I feel I've vanished in the forest, become part of the breath of that silent plantation. I don't care about the rise and fall of rubber prices on the global market. But suddenly my eyes see the figure of Sindi hugging the corpse of her uncle Bugu, like the toppling of an oral literature that can't refuse its mortal destiny. Sindi is alone. I don't know where her mother and little sister are.

I keep walking towards Sindi. I can hear her weeping. Sindi recognises my presence through a wet face while still hugging her uncle's corpse.

She glares at me:

"It was you who set off that riot!" she screams, pointing at me.

"Delete me from this shitty story of yours! Delete me immediately!"

Sindi doesn't know:

"I'm-on-ly-a-ca-me-ra!"

THE TOPPLING OF THE LETTER "F"

THE TOPPLING OF THE LETTER "F"

The Stars Are Making Shells On My Back

The hot dry season sun has turned my gaze a yellowish green. This is the colour I see when I look at something at night.

The yellowish green arrived tonight as a fresh wind blew from the sea, like a fan spinning in my lungs. White bed sheets trawled the air, as if wanting to replace the dense foliage of the remaining old trees by the edge of the road. Merauke: like the grace of Dela Gepze who once sent me a card at the end of Ramadan. Like the smile of Bony Mekiuw, who made white sand move from Anggayo beach to the skin on my back, where stars are making shells.

The Marind people, the Asmat people, government people, the police and the general populace filled the streets between the church and the pastor's house that night. My eyes were like fish flapping in a river run dry, a long dry season that had turned everything into dense mud. Speeches, dances and songs took turns occupying the stage. The party was in full swing: the 25th anniversary of the Bishop of Merauke, a silver anniversary, they said. I moved through the swirl of the crowd and the grandeur of church songs.

From beyond the stage came the sound of drum beats. Over there, on the main road. My feet began to move, looking for the origins of that sound. My yellowish green eyes saw troupes of Asmat people squatting at the edge of the road, avoiding the lights. Some of the women only wore bras and tasseled skirts. They had white marks on their bodies and faces; marks that embodied their culture.

My camera captured a cockroach twitching its antennae. Its blackish brown colour shone in the neon lights emanating from the church terrace. Five Marind people were bouncing while playing small drums. Their movements resembled dogs jumping behind a gate. I followed them, leaving the crowd, until I found myself in front of a dark and quiet building.

They wore whatever clothes had come their way. No colourful weavings or bright beads like those worn onstage. Some wore t-shirts bearing the emblems of various political parties. The t-shirts were threadbare and had faded to an indistinct brown.

They began to collect rubbish and burn it in front of the dark and quiet building. An icon of Mary cast a long shadow in front of the church, separated by a fence and a bicycle leaning against it. The people began to dance again amid the flames rising from the burning rubbish, immersed in the icon's shadow and surrounded by sharp fragments of light cast by neon bulbs.

The beating of the drums introduced a sensitivity to the night in front of the dark and quiet building. The night became a heart, a wilderness illuminat-

THE STARS ARE MAKING SHELLS ON MY BACK

ed under a sky full of stars. One of them suddenly hopped on one foot in the direction of the fire. There were shards of glass in his feet. The dancer put his drum down and approached the flames. He shed the t-shirt with the symbol of the political party and wrapped it around the wound on his foot. Then he resumed drumming and dancing. It was the Eng-gatzi Dance; a dog dance of the Marind people, who had largely isolated themselves from the party. They had chosen quietness. They didn't feel themselves to be part of that grandeur; they felt distant from the shiny fabric and beads of the dancers on the stage.

Through the fan spinning in my lungs, between bedsheets catching the wind, a figure resembling Jesus glided down from above, gently swaying like the branches of a melaleuca tree before landing on the ground beside me. Everything was complete, whole, a golden green kind of colour. The delicate night was complete too. The earth I was standing on splintered. The splinters got caught in the soles of my feet and the palms of my hands. The earth looking for a different church and a different Freeport. A hungry Weimena; Timika guarded by soldiers; give me a literary work from my own people.

The night became a golden green. Over there. Like moss on fragments of gold. The land of the Marind people has been siphoned off by newcomers; like a snake suckling a cow's teat.

I couldn't move any further. The jungle was guarded by soldiers. I didn't have permission to enter. In the village of Namen, a journey from the centre of the city which passed through black scorched earth and charcoal trees, I was stopped in my tracks by shouting coming from inside the village. The shouts were from the throat of a man drowning in stones: "Is there a nation here?" A shouting which rearranged the silence of the village into sensitivity. Houses of wood and tin turned the sun into a giant metal disc above my head. There weren't any roofs made from the bark of the melaleuca tree.

Bony Mekiuw suddenly arrived and dragged me through the Wasur jungle. He took me further into the jungle. A jungle where only leaves and stars occupied the skies. In the middle of that jungle sky, I encountered some Marind people performing the Enggatzi dance. They smiled at me with fierce eyes. Eyes that reminded me of parched rivers of dense mud choking fish in the dry season. Oblivion in a river; a banal death not far from my neck.

I danced with them. I played the drum while shouting "Eaaaa!" My voice echoed through the melaleuca trees. Something was happening; as though a tension building for 300 years, since foreign ships first arrived on this island, was being released. My skin became black and my bones swelled. My jaw and cheek bones became more pronounced, more severe.

Through my eyes, I saw the forest change, like a cow's abdominal cavity hung in an abattoir. They began to call me "Yowel Mekiuw". From that day on I lived as one of them. After the UNTEA administration. After so much had been taken from this land.

Heavy rain had fallen, and several parts of Jakarta were flooded. The flood had washed the rubbish from the streets into houses. I didn't care for this. My legs were reluctant to touch the rubbish infested water; it felt slimy and stunk. I knew that the next day, residents' yards would be filled with items being cleaned and dried following the floods.

It was then that I received a letter from Dela Gepze. He told a long story about the fate of Yowel Mekiuw who continued to shut himself away in the forest. He refused to eat rice, relying instead on sago as his staple food. The kind of food that made the bones in his body swell. Yowel refused to live in a zinc roofed house because it would turn the sun into a metal disk above his head.

Yowel began to write poetry, retelling the myths of the origins of his people; myths born from a dog, pig, coconut and sago plant. A computer he had once brought back from Jakarta was now being used as a table. He wrote his poetry on bark on that table. The myths brought him closer to the natural world around him. He didn't experience a great ontological distance between himself and dogs, pigs, the sago plant or a coconut. All were part of him.

He was of the habit of reading his poems aloud in the forest beside a campfire as midnight approached. When he read, it was as though the crashing of the waves of Anggayo beach were audible in his throat. The stars made shells on his back. The Marind people encircled him. That morning on a street corner... the sunlight suddenly appeared.

The stars of the gods fell supine. City officials began smashing penis gourds and black beads. Whose side were the gods on? The morning was hurled to the ground. It held nothing but sorrow in its chest.[*]

Fragments of gold, tree trunks, uranium, tin, and coal were churning in the Earth's stomach. Gaping, like a cow's abdominal cavity hanging in an abattoir.

Dela Gepze cried in his letter. He spoke of an arrow that one day pierced Yowel Mekiuw's stomach. No one knew who shot him with the arrow. The tip of the arrow smelt of kerosene. The sand and shells fell from his back. Yowel bled as he removed the arrow lodged in his back. The stars continued to make shells around the arrow protruding from his back. The arrow told Yowel he couldn't return to the natural world of his ancestors. The forest had been buried in a cow's abdominal cavity hanging in an abattoir.

My gaze was still tinged golden green. The conflict between the forest and city life raged without respite. Cassowaries, kangaroos and towering termite mounds were toppled, becoming mere ornaments for the city people.

A transformation that spread like a plague. The Marind people who encircled Yowel Mekiuw transformed into a pig, golden green. Their bodies smelt of coal and oil. A hungry pig. Yowel crawled towards the pig. Expelled blood from his back in order to approach that hungry pig. Dela Gepze cried once more. Yowel raised his hands before that hungry pig. Then another part of Yowel's body, like a great thundering church chorus, like love moving through time, was devoured by the pig.

[*]Quoted from a poem by Cannon, a poet from Manokwari who was productive during the first half of the 1980s. "That Morning on the Street Corner" (*Horison*, No.2, February, 1981).

Since then, the forest has fallen silent. The sky stunk. I walked alone looking for Yowel Mekiuw with a fan spinning in my lungs. The forest turned a golden green colour. A foreign feeling, the smell of a chainsaw. A golden liquid dripped from fragments of stones.

The night darkened. The forest was a shining black mirror. I stepped on a cassowary egg. The green egg was empty. The smell of Yowel Mekiuw wafted from the egg. I knew I couldn't kill Yowel Mekiuw. I was the one who'd shot him with the arrow. I was trying to bring his quest to rediscover the past, a past which had already been smashed to smithereens, to an end.

My feet approached the river. The cold wind gripped my neck tightly, darkness smothering my face. In the distance I saw a shaft of light piercing the golden green fog. The light came from a boat. The boat moved slowly along the river towards me. The fan in my lungs spun faster; like the tears of Dela Gepze. The light, the boat, neared, landing at the edge of the river. The shells on my back multiplied.

The golden green fog blanketed the boat as it came to rest amid the shrubbery by the river bank. The sound of trickling water rose to my earlobe. A hand clasped me and pulled me into the boat. A hand of love. Like golden green fog. I smelled Jesus in that boat; just like the smell of Yowel Mekiuw, struck by the arrow. A red odour.

The sun will shine again tomorrow. Like remembering the grace of Dela Gepze, who still waits for Yowel Mekiuw to emerge from the forest. But Dela doesn't know that Yowel will never come home. He has returned to the forest forever. The boat continued upstream, the golden green fog. The stars kept making shells on my back, as though delivering traces of Yowel from the sea.

Attempt
at
Making
an
Ear

I was awoken by the shadow of a black man pray-
ing in front of a television set. A face that wants to
visit your life. Refamiliarise itself with the presence
of blood; with a godliness that awaits you on the
inside, permanently.

It was nine in the morning. The television was
still on. The lights in the room were still on. I was
buried in my blanket. Cold air inhabited the mattress. I tried to get up, turn off the lights and television and open the curtains. It was drizzling outside.
I remembered the news story from CNN last night.
Demonstrators were marching before the Welcome
Statue, below the Hotel Indonesia.

A friend from Germany called. He was distressed
to see armoured vehicles built by his own country
blocking the demonstrators. Eternal drivers drove
vehicles belonging to the past, looking for temporal
estuaries in the present.

But the drizzle is another country. I readied
myself without having a shower. Abandoned the
verbal assault of words which never amount to
anything. I went down to the restaurant and had
breakfast. Two slices of bread entered my stomach.
One glass of orange juice and an unfinished cup of

coffee. The knife with the remnants of butter on it shined.

In the wide plate glass window of the restaurant, my eyes were like a self-focusing camera lens. People strode briskly in the drizzle. Living inside themselves. The shops began to open. The city felt polite. Didn't immodestly flaunt itself. I barely heard a sound.

"Afrizal!" Suddenly I heard a greeting. A once familiar greeting from 100 years ago. Now it was here. The greeting made me feel like a new person; my synapses opened to memories and other redundant information.

"Ogaga!" We greeted each other. His hand was black, like the rest of his body. He had thick lips, which drooped a little. His gaze was somehow occupied by sadness, extreme self-confidence and an enormous desire to be friends. He was wearing long sleeves. He was about ten years younger than me.

"Indonesia... One day I want to hear it from you." His voice was heavy. This poet from Nigeria then took his leave. He seemed busy. I didn't know what was keeping him busy. He left, but it was as though a part of him stayed. He left it to keep me company while I drank my coffee.

The drizzle tried to reformulate me into various concepts. A line from one of his poems accompanied me, "We distance ourselves from sickness and write lyrics from ears," he had written.

Why did he deploy the ear like that? Maybe he no longer trusted the mouth. A rubbish bin for words. But truly, there is no poverty in this city, or bullshit.

ATTEMPT AT MAKING AN EAR

A city that was destroyed during World War Two. Now, it's developing a new face, making it very different from the surrounding cities.

In a room, in the de Doelen building, I met Ogaga again. It was as if he didn't recognise me. His face was dull. His thick lips appeared to droop much lower than before. He was wearing black sunglasses and a shirt from Nigeria with intricate patterns. His self confidence had gone, submerged deeply within his appearance. He wore new shoes. Made from leather. They seemed very long and pointy. I felt it was surely too short a period of time for him to have lost himself. It had been only three hours since our meeting in the restaurant.

I met him again in a café in front of the Schouwburg theatre. He was with a young black woman. He introduced her to me. She had been living in the city for a long time and came from Rwanda. A nation riddled with bloody ethnic conflict. She was wearing black clothes and a jacket made from leather.

I didn't care for the idea that the woman might have been born of Ogaga's ear. That ear appeared to store a black sky. A universe painted completely black. Rejecting blood. Anything could happen. I won't understand if the miracles end here.

From the wide plate glass window, I saw a large flock of birds combing the sky. As though they were heading to another country.

In the hotel lobby, I met Ogaga again. He was sitting with two suitcases beside him. "Afrizal, we are parting," he said with the same warmth he had exuded the first time I met him. He gave me two addresses: one in Germany and one in Nigeria. His jacket appeared brand new.

"*Tschüss*, Ogaga," I said.

Birds were flying in front of the old palace. There was a wax museum there, containing the statues of various famous people. It was as though my vision was split by a fault line within time that existed somewhere in that city. An old city populated with new people from various nations. The canals encircling this city created cycles that we'll meet again, elsewhere.

The wind was cold. A busker performed a pantomime in front of the shops. I ordered some fried chips with sour sauce. The church bells rang out. I saw Ogaga sitting beneath one of the city's clocktowers eating a boiled egg. He let the crumbling eggshell drop to the ground. He saw me, as though seeing a bird caught in a trap.

Ogaga dropped off the stoop and approached me. The cold wind made his eyes red and watery. His mouth was still a black sky, and his trembling voice arrived from a hundred years ago. I wanted to fly into that black sky. My body was like cracked eggshells.

I wanted to peel it off.

It was a brighter day than yesterday. We sat on the edge of a canal in front of the train station. Ogaga was wearing traditional clothes from his country. His body was covered with primitive symbols. He sang songs of his ancestors. People took no notice of us on the edge of the canal.

I was wearing a long, light dress. It was creamy

white in colour, and made from silk. I wore black-ish green coloured high heel shoes. My long hair blew in the wind. I felt younger and more beautiful than usual. The flesh of my face felt fresher without make-up. The tourist boat passed before me, like a chocolate filled toy.

Ogaga fumbled with his passport. "This is a nation," he said. His face was gloomy and cynical. His body smelled of dusty dry earth. "In my country," he said, "there is an animal which covers the roads with rifles. But that animal doesn't know, despair is an enormous convoy immune to a barrage of bullets. That animal frequently pollutes its own drinking water, enters its neighbours' houses, kidnaps children as they sleep, and enjoys the sound of sirens. That animal is strong. That animal can't die. The animal can only die of suicide."

Ogaga got up. As if the story was going to suffocate. Suddenly, he dived into the water. He was under for a while. I waited for several minutes but he didn't come up. I didn't like this game. Death was no prospect for the story he had just told about the animal.

I got up and walked away from the canal. I left a cigarette and my lighter behind at the edge of the canal. If Ogaga re-emerged from his long dive, which may have taken him beyond his own death, he might be feeling cold and need a cigarette, although he wasn't a smoker.

After Ogaga disappeared, strange fur began sprouting from my skin. I could smell meat. Or perhaps it was more like the smell of a down blanket.

I tried to forget all about this by occupying myself with new activities. I paid particular attention to the sky and the grayness reflected on the surface of the canal. I even started to like this city. It was like a 15ᵗʰ century city occupied by people from the present. An old city that had been given electricity and various other technological ameliorations. The city was denser than others.

As I was ordering a ticket at the train station, a black man asked me for a cigarette. I gave him one. But my desire to fulfill the man's request disrupted everything. I didn't buy a train ticket.

Several moments later I found myself busy in a shop looking for a book. I wanted to buy *Feminist Theatre* by Helene Keyssar. I recognised a photograph of a performance called *Steaming* depicting a number of women in a sauna wrapped in towels.

I remembered the fur growing on my body. That fur began to sway gently, as if there was an animal beneath it. I placed the book down in its original position. When I was alone like this, I doubted whether I was still a woman. I picked another book off the shelf. There were lots of performance photographs in it. They were replicating the lives of angels.

I liked it. I can't describe my happiness upon finding this book. It wasn't important whether or not I was a human being. I felt a new kind of existence without identity. Approaching the final page, I saw a photograph of Ogaga. It was yellowish and out of focus. A pair of wings were affixed to his back, taller than his body.

His body looked small between the two great

ATTEMPT AT MAKING AN EAR

wings. The wings almost reached the ground. His lips were thick and drooping. There was no more stench of blood.

"Dynana Kukama!" he greeted me with the same 100 year old voice. Perhaps my name had changed. It was the same one I had in my passport. I was a storyteller born in South Africa. My skin had turned black. My hair had fine curls and was tied in small plaits with colourful beads at the end.

Ogaga began to play the violin. People in the bookshop took an interest in Ogaga's performance. They clapped. But I could see something harsh in their eyes. People didn't understand that his playing was an effort to oppose such harshness, harshness emanating from weapons stored in history books for all eternity.

I closed the book, like assassinating someone behind a door. The church bells rang out. The sound produced the impression of a vast open space, growing exponentially in size as the bells reverberated. The air felt humid; like washing before it dries. As though something was floating inside my body, trying to find a way out.

Several days later, I found myself in a quiet village surrounded by wheat fields. There was a windmill, bloated and short. It emitted a strange sound, like it was pressing a living creature deep into the earth, drowning it.

Ogaga walked beside me with the wings on his back. My body was sprouting the same wings. I played with them while walking like a pig. Sometimes like a seahorse screaming in pain. Ogaga laughed at my antics. My wings shed some feathers.

"The wheat fields remind me of my home village," he said. "Bitter houses like crying eyes, walls buttressed by fear. Our beds and the roofs of our homes have become plaintive ballads; expressing elegies and dreams of murder. Truth, it turns out, is made from weapons, knives and a congress of words."

I began to understand why Ogaga wanted to write poems from ears. On his prominent earlobe, I saw another sky. A sky reeking of blood. Silvery shafts of light tinged the sky. We'd become a pair of birds. Flying. Higher. Entering clumps of silvery black storm clouds. Entering an ear which wanted to hear a whole spectrum of sound.

The television was still on. The lights in the room were still on. The curtains were closed; shutting themselves off from the drizzle outside. The ghosts in the hotel room no longer reeked of blood. The television shed feathers like snowflakes.

Note: The majority of Ogaga's dialogue in this short story has been reconstructed from various poems by Ogaga Ifowodo, a Nigerian poet.

The Fish Market in Aquarium

The fish market by the mouth of the Ciliwung River in North Jakarta, blew like an old jaundiced wind. Boat lines, anchors, nets and baskets were dragged about. The fish market was a giant morgue. Like a membrane, reordering the fluids of my brain into a different structure. The sea breeze turned the ship masts into an imperceptible clot of time.

Not far from the market was a ghostly old Dutch colonial building. There were prison cells beneath it, dark and waterlogged. A man was selling dried squid in a basket. He wore a faded jacket and a necklace. His hair and beard united in a sequence of thin tight curls. Only his mustache appeared thick, black and stout. He claimed to be from Trier, a small city in West Germany. The viscous fluid in my mouth began to move, like oil particles clinging to the estuary breakwater.

The fluid reminded me of the warm smell of burnt hair and a public decree from the summer of a different era: "Verboden voor Inlanders!" – "Forbidden for Natives!" A statement once known intimately. The decree was attached to certain buildings in the colonial era. Those words didn't just exhibit entrenched power, but also a fatal anthropology engulfing the natives.

The words were those of a native. A native equated with the sound of coughing in the night. The words were written in a place where people could be woken up early in the morning. A watery affliction. Constantly wet. From a portion of head surrounded by fish. It resembled the aquarium in your house.

I left the fish market for good last rainy season. But from time to time I still hear the native's cough. Like the corpse of a microphone on a portion of head surrounded by fish. It contained many relations. Stones were scattered around it. Grass and concrete. The foul military boots of the Japanese, samurai swords and the neglected bones of time.

There was another man there. He was wearing shorts and sandals. He was laughing, as though laughing at his own reality. He had a small body. His name was Sjahrir. He had a sweet and symmetrical face. But his face was encircled by fish. He gathered the stones scattered about the yard of the building where the National Committee assembled.

Each stone he gathered made fish heads tremble. The water in the aquarium became turbid, the lives of the fish shrieked. Behold, I rearrange myself with the sound of coughing and the same body odour. A self built of the paradox of the Third World; a paradox which incorporates rationality and sorcery, heroes and scoundrels, independence and insanity, love and naked desire.

"Time is a vehicle." I have no idea where this concept suddenly came from. I'd encountered it before. It was full of tension, impatience and fear. Vulnerable to various prejudices.

Some people still recall the presence of a time like that. The Japanese surrendered to the Allies. Independence was proclaimed. The aquarium was rocked by all the tension and hope produced over hundreds of years. It was to be resolved instantaneously, just as the Declaration of Independence proposed to "transfer power in the shortest possible time."

The text was like a mantra capable of repatriating all the time which had been stolen. The political organisations and the people's brigades which sprouted were the biological children of the quickest transfer possible. They displayed their revolutionary character as if emerging from the middle of the forest. Combined with street thugs bearing talismans. They had a base, tactics and the authority to determine who were enemy spies. There were kidnappings everywhere.

Time had been packed up, the old décor deconstructed by that transfer of power. Fish jumped out of the aquarium. Brain fluids floated on the surface of the water, creating unguarded moments of courage. It was as though people were seeing the sunrise for the first time, destroying all the buildings which got in their way. Radicalism emerged behind the shadows of the bared teeth of the past, wounded and full of misunderstandings.

"This is the first time we've had a cabinet in all this time. A cabinet!" I shouted. My ancestors had never known such a thing.

The assembly to decide on the composition of the independence government went for hours, days. It was drenched in anxiety and attended by red eyes that hadn't rested in weeks. I clearly remember your nose, which frequently bore beads of sweat, and the smell of cheap tobacco. The meeting swallowed time, and still no conclusion was reached. The attendees got increasingly anxious. A minister was talking to himself in Dutch, fretting about the spilling of blood. Every now and then he pulled up his sagging trousers. He looked hungry.

The assembly reminded me of the anxious smell of your body. Your sentences were crude and came from a weary political language. A tense ideology came to inhabit the way you looked at me. I still recognised the slices of your head in the aquarium, the fragments of fish bodies scattered along the northern coast. And the pure mute emotions of a native.

One of the participants on the committee threatened to open fire, shouting at the other participants whom he mistrusted: "Are you fascists?"

Fascism. He feared fascism and militarism. A totalitarian government, a homeland prone to insanity. "The world is tired of war and spilt blood. America and England are the new capitalist powers, leading their allies in war. Democracy has become the new language." Sjahrir deliberated over thoughts like these while sitting on the floor of an empty building. The Japanese had removed all the furniture.

That big empty building is a desolate image by which to repeat your question: what can be achieved by this transfer of power in the shortest possible time? A riot? Money and expertise, the same as shouting, "I have been expelled from the group". The furniture has all been confiscated. Our guests have taken everything and put the slices of my head inside an aquarium. Sjahrir's thoughts are as empty as that unfurnished building.

The stones leave a damp residue. But the man with fish on his head is feverishly insisting on issuing a political decree. So the world knows: "This republic is founded on democracy, not fascism." The alarm clock strikes even faster in the aquarium, every occurrence rearranging the stones.

You condemn that step as opening the door to Americanisation, just like earlier critiques in the form of imperialism. The beads of sweat on your nose start to smell of cigars, alcohol and Marilyn Monroe's underwear. The fish move in search of different currents. But the Republic must obtain the world's trust that it is not being ruled by Japanese collaborators. Japan is fascist, just like the blade in my trouser pocket.

Sjahrir's cabinet takes over from the previous cabinet. You could smell the stench of your burnt hair when the Company returned with the Allies. It's as though I'm remembering the city of your birth: its kampungs bombed by the Dutch in the afternoons. At night, buildings and big houses were burnt to the ground. A banana tree behind your house was felled, and fragments of a goat's body were catapulted into your decrepit well. Retaliations were carried out across Java, and brave slogans emerged, too:

"Van Mook!"

"Van der Plas!"

"What are you doing here?!"

The dock workers at Tanjung Priok went on strike. Other workers refused to serve Europeans. The city of the Proclamation suffered rice shortages. Kerawang staged a boycott. But the anti-Republic movement kept pace, and pamphlets were spread voicing criticisms: "Japanese souls in Indonesian bodies live on within the Republic."

I'd often see that bearded man swinging between ship masts. Every now and then, he accompanied me in my sleep. His body smelt of fruits and burnt copper. The corpses of microphones crowded my head in ever greater numbers.

"Time," I thought, "is maybe just a fable. And gecko shit on the wall."

Once again, the dry season was over. The fish in that aquarium knew that politics smells of burnt plastic. The new cabinet was liberalising everything. Parties were born of primordial ties. At the same time, the world was rearranging itself; nuclear power and the formation of a global market; existentialism and Marilyn Monroe, Marxism and rock'n'roll.

War changed a lot of things. It disrupted the way I look at you; like dried fish hung at the Fish Market. I saw the bearded man from Trier sitting by the mouth of the Ciliwung. He was holding something. An aquarium in the form of a glass jar. In that aquarium were the heads of Tan Malaka and Musso; made from the materialism of a ship's engine oil. Red ants gathered around the remaining fish bones.

The sky above unfurled as though it was time's moving vehicle. Old and jaundiced. A vehicle which gave birth to many tragic figures.

The cabinet didn't last long, just like other cabinets after Sjahrir's time. There was increasing polarisation. The nation became weaker. Several regions no longer wanted to support the centre. They rebelled. Sjahrir was arrested. His party was disbanded. The aquarium in his head was confiscated. The angels took it to a foreign nation full of flowers and snow capped mountain ranges lying like peaceful cows above churches and bicycles. He died in a foreign country.

After his death, I often gazed at the head in the aquarium. It felt cold, and life was too hot. I tried to understand a lonely foreign death, surrounded by encircling fish; how political modernity rolled on, without a sufficient rational basis. The paradox of a chicken coop in a house, and a grave that demands prophecies. The aquarium reeked of meat; meat in need of brain fluid.

"I need knowledge and technology. Not power!"

The fish didn't want to be turned into plastic. In the cabinet meeting underway at the Bogor Palace, I brought the aquarium filled with slices of my head. One of the participants was angry. He raised the table, preparing to throw it. My head fell out of the aquarium. The stench of burnt hair filled the room. Fish writhed in the meeting's microphone. The leader of the meeting, Sukarno, forcefully pounded his gavel and made a decision:

"I declare this session closed. What has taken

place here cannot be mentioned outside."

More was said following this declaration, but all I could make out was a political language full of fists. The aquarium walls fell silent. The voices that vanished made a part of time move with silent steps. Steps which could suddenly smother you from behind, leaving an uncertain fate. A kind of time monster, walking in the hallways of the nation.

The dry season arrived again. I needed to breathe in cleaner air. A kind of commonsense. The fish in my head skirted the walls of the aquarium, trying to hear the beating of time there, wanting to smell the salty air.

The bearded man from Trier still stood by the mouth of the Ciliwung River. A dense black fluid inundated the estuary. The market would soon close. Sunset arrived like steel particles falling on ship masts. The man from Trier offered me a watch.

"It's from Moscow," he said.

I saw something engraved on the watch.

"The Party is dead."

The old jaundiced wind blew again. Reminding me of a cold and constrained heart. Fragile and un-protected. The heart of a person who did not die in his own country. "I love this country and its people. Mainly because I've always known them as people who suffer. Defeated people. Ordinary people. I have sympathy for underdogs. Those who are oppressed."

It is night in the aquarium. The filter cleans the muck inside it. The bubbles sound like an angel's breath on the glass walls.

I drag myself away from the Fish Market. Noth-

ing has changed on those ships' masts by the mouth
of the Ciliwung; the unseen fangs of time. It is quiet.
I see a man talking on a public telephone. He is
bald.

Feet of Water

Since the floods last month, which drowned the governor in the Ciliwung river, never to be found again, the city's roads have become unbearably potholed. The people of the city have nightmares about the governor's death and the holes in the main roads.

The people celebrated his death as the death of a monster. An exorcism was carried out at Sunda Kelapa port. The people prayed on top of a boat, purifying the souls tortured throughout the governor's reign. They also held a ceremony in order to bring the meaning of communal life back to their kampungs. But this city is a ferocious melting pot. The shop houses form walls, as though they are the city's fences. They also happen to be made of highly flammable timber ready to hand whenever riots break out.

A mother taking her child to school must jump from one car roof to the next to cross the traffic jammed roads. A cyclist surmounts obstacles by jumping from one bus to the next. Children play basketball on the Depok-Kota train line. Oh, Jakarta, you are like a young lady with swollen calves: full of sardines, sausages and butter.

I bought the morning paper. This city is always

161

full of news. The vice president has seven wives. The president has been taken hostage on video. Trillions of dollars are spent in a single day. The stock market rises and falls. Everyone's been doing crack at the vice governor of West Java's place. The American Embassy is closed and the price of flour is going up. A young man who stole some beans was beaten up by the masses. Some members of a political party have been ostracised, and their voices won't be heard in an upcoming gubernatorial election. But, the governor up for re-election has died in the aforementioned floods. A heroin syndicate has been caught. Suddenly a bus came out of the newspaper I was reading. The conductor shouted:

"Grogol!"

"Grogol!"

"You have to be polite in public!"

Goddamn, how do people live the good life in this city? People are little more than sources of tax, aren't they? Citizens are just whatever parts of this city can be extorted.

Don't worry too much. Quality is unimportant. What matters is unencumbered daily transactions, no? And in a nightmare, giving meaning to one's life via darkness is one way of filling the void left by various outlandish attempts to establish quality of life just so that life may go on.

It's incumbent upon me to correct the lies in the morning paper. In truth, I do not buy or read the newspaper. What's more, those stories have never existed. That morning, I was sweeping the front yard.

I was pruning the plants and watering them. The shrubs wouldn't let up about their roots which were smarting from lack of water. The mango tree was itchy all over because it was covered in white fungus. But what was the difference? A bus suddenly emerged from a mound of earth. The conductor shouted:

"Grogol!"

"Grogol!"

"You have to be polite in public!"

The sun had just unentangled itself from a tall fence topped with barbed wire. The city felt quieter than usual. There were few vehicles on the streets. More people were choosing to stay home. A lot of offices and trading areas were closed. Something was happening.

Two days ago, several potholes in the city streets suddenly became deep wells of clear water. Unknown species of fish swam in the wells.

My son Jilan would visit the wells twice daily just to peer down into them. When he came home from looking at the wells, I'd see that his eyes had also become a pair of deep wells with clear water and previously unknown fish. The plague of wells spread quickly: millions of people's eyes turned into deep wells with clear water and previously undiscovered fish.

The creatures with eyes like wells transformed the everyday life of the city. The creatures with eyes like wells soon experienced a second symptom; the wells disguised an unexpected power. When a

163

motorised vehicle passed the wells, its engine would abruptly die. Only motorless vehicles were able to pass. The same applied for those citizens whose eyes had become wells; electronic goods died as soon as they cast eyes upon them.

Many electronic goods and motorised vehicles suddenly died in this city. Those whose eyes hadn't become wells were suddenly highly prized, worthy of protection status. They were deployed in key positions to keep the city running. They were escorted wherever they went. There were several methods employed to protect them. If anyone disrupted the activity of these highly prized citizens, they were shot on the spot.

The city government thought long and hard about how to close the wells that had materialised throughout the city. This was no easy task to solve, because a steady stream of tears was gushing from those who strove to close the wells. Theirs were tears that nothing could stop. Deep and sorrowful tears. Tears that evoked great sadness among those who heard the wailing.

People no longer spoke of the minutiae of their daily lives. Since the wells emerged, city residents were more likely to discuss the meaning of love and time. Who knows why these two topics came to occupy the minds of residents.

Those whose eyes weren't transformed into wells were not exempt from this change in topic of conversation. They also began debating the meaning of love and time. They neglected their roles in running the city because they were more interested in getting to the bottom of these two topics. Those tasked with minding them did nothing to prevent this state of affairs. They were powerless to stop people from discussing the meaning of love and time. There was no law forbidding it. The guards themselves were frequently spellbound listening to people talk about love and time.

That tune caused the sky to emit a blue light at night. People were deeply touched by this change. They felt they had a new relationship with the sky. Watching the sky at night was like watching creatures whose job was to knit time and love into a vast quilt.

The songs of love and time were heard everywhere. Many people composed songs about these topics. The songs and the wells abruptly transformed the city into a very romantic place. People started to plant flowers and sew their own clothes, as if knitting time for their future.

"Look, now I believe! Now I feel alive!"

"I'm alive, aren't I?" they shouted.

It was as if their bodies were filled with fresh blood. Their old blood, thick and dirty, had evaporated who knows where. Their old skins, dull and deathly from the pollution in the city, were replaced with new skin, soft and smooth. Their lips were no longer chapped and blue. Their lips were like succulent red tomatoes. They lived like plants. "Look... there's a tomato... there's a carrot... there's a chili... there's... everything! Every kind of plant is here!" said Princess.

"*Morgen*, Princess, my dear."

The city no longer chased helter-skelter after the machine producing speed at double time. The movements of the city's residents became normal, natural. Time also passed normally, no longer out of step with human reason. Bodily gestures were no longer tense and stiff. People walked as if they were dancing. Their lips were always poised to say something friendly. Their clothes were... it was as if they contained a prayer house within them... a place to make love.

One day, I don't know who started it, the residents started planting trees in the city's potholed streets. Trees that bore fruit. The city's main thoroughfares became urban forests. A forest nurtured by those wells and by the peoples' hands. City taxes were used by the people to build their city that now stood transformed.

"Father, I want to be a street cleaner," said Jilan. You laughed upon hearing this, a laughter saturated in a way of interpreting what's right and proper. Love no longer needs to carry a knife in its hand. Love is the promise I utter to every grain of rice I eat, every drop of water I drink, and every breath of air I inhale. Love is... wells creating time from the feet of water.

10th September, 2002, Kalimalang

Bottle
Headed
Ghost

One night.

Why one night?

That night, my neighbour pounded on the door of my house. I woke up startled. My neighbour was a woman whose husband had left her. She lived with her child and worked as a street vendor. The oil on her face shone beneath the fluorescent light emanating from my house. She seemed jittery and tired. It was clear from her expression that she couldn't take in what was going on around her. I guessed she was about 37 years old.

"Do you have some medicine for an upset stomach? My child is sick," she said.

She wore a sarong and a cardigan without the buttons done up.

"I don't have any medicine," I said, pondering where it would be possible to buy some.

It was night, after all.

The woman began to cry and left.

"Where are you going?"

"To find some medicine. Right now."

Right now.

"Bloody hell." I didn't know who I should be angry with. Why did her child have to be sick? Why did it have to be night? It was almost midnight. My neck felt stiff. Could a dog be turned into medicine? If it could, I would go find a dog.

Right now.

It was almost midnight.

I remembered her child. She was awake. I entered their house. Why wasn't it locked? Because there was a small girl with a stomach problem. But what if someone had bad intentions? Why would someone do something nasty?

Inside the house I saw her child sound asleep. The night didn't belong to anyone; except that child. Her breath was calm and soft. Her lips indicated a hidden joy.

Who really had the stomach problem? This child was not sick. She was beautiful. I had never seen such beauty. A girl who seemed to be singing and dancing in her sleep. Maybe people are only beautiful when they're sleeping. But people also get stomach problems. Wasn't that the case? Where had her mother gone? It was already past midnight.

A dog howled outside. If medicine could be made from a dog to treat a stomach problem, I would put the dog in the mouth of the beautiful small girl. And I would feel the life shining from her beautiful body, her dancing and singing. The meat of the dog would heat her cold and damp stomach up. The meat of the dog would absorb the poison making her sick.

But, that child was beautiful, not sick. Yes, she wasn't sick. Or, did her mother think that beauty was a kind of sickness? Who knows? Perhaps that's how she sees it. Maybe she needs medicine for beauty.

Huh?

If so, then a dog is truly the only medicine. But why a dog? Where does this idea of a dog as medicine come from? The howling dog was heard once more. A howling which made the night seem as though it was dragging a corpse along the edge of the city.

Suddenly the door opened. The mother of the daughter came in and embraced me.

"There is no medicine," she said. "There is no medicine for a stomach problem."

She bit my ear. Then she hurriedly took off all her clothes as if she was about to take a shower.

Was I a bathroom?

She tore my clothes off. Wrapped herself up in me as if I were a towel. The howling of the dog reverberated from the lower floor, from under the ground, from the middle of the earth. My navel exuded an oily sweat. She fucked me as if she was stabbing a dagger into the mattress. The howls of the dog could now be heard from my navel.

My brow was wounded from her bites. Dog claws emerged from the wounds. Flames came out of her vagina. Blue flames. Flames like tears. My penis was scorched inside her. Metal and rocks began to melt. Night was like an open coffin.

I could see a desire trying to give birth to a new universe in the cavity of her mouth. My entire body was entering that universe. A universe which emitted warm air and the sound of her child's singing.

Only my shadow remained outside, trembling on the floor without me.

The girl who was sleeping suddenly convulsed. Her hips rose, making her body form an arc. Her muscles tensed. Suddenly an arseless bottle was ejected from her stomach. The bottle flew out the window.

Then the child died; her beauty died.

The pharmacy has been closed for three months. The only pharmacy in the little town where I live. Since then, it's been difficult to find medicine in this town. People have to go to other cities to find medicine.

The pharmacy in my town has been closed ever since a riot took place inside. One night, the pharmacy was turned upside down by an arseless bottle which went on a riot and destroyed everything in that pharmacy. People called this phantom the arseless bottle headed ghost. No one knew where the ghost came from nor why it trashed the pharmacy.

One of the chemists who worked in the pharmacy said the bottle had been around for quite some time. Apparently, the bottle had once been used to store blood. Whose blood? Did the blood have a name?

The ghost of the arseless bottle also started riots in the pharmacies of the city closest to where I lived. It pulverised all the medicine. It made humans feel immortal in ill health until death came and claimed their souls. It was as if the ghost wanted to prove that there was no medicine that could cure a sick human being. Hello... hello... sickness and death are part of our daily lives.

Now, every night, it's as if a dog howls from my ear. The people in my kampung are determined to

170

catch the arseless ghost with the bottle for a head. They carry among them a keris and various metallic weapons made in Kuningan. Several people who know about these things announce that only weapons made in Kuningan are appropriate for catching ghosts. Weapons that are untainted and have never been used to kill anything.

"Why has an arseless bottle made us all panicky like this?" This was the tone of the frequent conversations that took place in the kampung.

"That ghost probably won't cause us any grief. Why should it? It's a ghost. Ghosts don't have any business with us, do they? Ghosts just tempt us to do something sinful."

"Maybe it's just encouraging us to remain vigilant."

"Huh?! The ghost of an arseless bottle is not a prophet!"

"This might be political."

"What kind of politics?"

"Anything around here can turn political, can't it?"

"You speak like an arseless bottle."

"Let's pray that the ghost doesn't come out of our own mouths."

One night, there was commotion in the kampung where I lived. People were shouting that the ghost of the arseless bottle had been caught. They chopped it to bits with the keris and the weapons from Kuningan.

Their faces were filled with a new hope. A new spirit, as if a new era were stretched out before them. The calamity had been brought to an end. That bastard situation caused by the ghost of the arseless bottle was over. Done. Their eyes shone with happiness and the prospect of a safe life without the ghost of an arseless bottle.

The next morning, everyone was mournful. All their hope and new spirit had disappeared. Their sadness made the sky appear potholed. As if life had frozen in my kampung. Residents' faces appeared strange and old. People didn't have the heart to greet each other, to say one another's names. Their souls were like a dark hole buried in a thicket. Hope never came to a dark and grieving soul.

The grief which had arrived came from the realisation that what the residents slaughtered the night before was not the ghost of an arseless bottle but a fellow kampung resident. This only became apparent as dawn broke in the kampung. That was when the ghost of the arseless bottle worked its dark magic on them. They killed one of their own neighbours.

"We were wrong," said one of them.

"We didn't interrogate it first. We didn't take it to court to have it sentenced. We merely replaced justice with weapons and violence. We made no effort to understand the motives of the ghost of the arseless bottle, destroyer of all the medicine in our city."

"Something is ruining our commonsense."

My neighbor pounded on the door of my house. I woke up startled. My neighbor was a man whose wife had left him. He lived with his child and worked as a street vendor. The oil on his face shone beneath the fluorescent light emanating from my house. He seemed jittery and tired. It was clear from his expression that he wasn't sure what was going on around him. I guessed he was about 37 years old.

"Do you have some medicine for an upset stomach? My child is sick," he said.

He wore a sarong and a cardigan without the buttons done up.

"I don't have any medicine," I said, pondering where it would be possible to buy some.

It was night, after all.

The man began to cry and left.

"Where are you going?"

"To find some medicine. Right now."

Right now.

"Bloody hell." I didn't know who I should be angry with. Why did his child have to be sick? Why did it have to be night? It was almost midnight. My neck felt stiff. Could a dog be turned into medicine? If it could, I would go find a dog.

Right now.

It was almost midnight.

I remembered his child. She was awake. I entered their house. Why wasn't it locked? Because there was a small girl with a stomach problem. But what if someone had bad intentions? Why would someone do something nasty?

Inside the house I saw his child sound asleep. The night didn't belong to anyone; except that child. Her breath was calm and soft. Her lips indicated a hidden joy.

Who really had the stomach problem? This child

was not sick. She was beautiful. I had never seen such beauty. A girl who seemed to be singing and dancing in her sleep. Maybe people are only beautiful when they're sleeping. But people also get stomach problems. Wasn't that the case? Where had her father gone? It was already past midnight.

A dog howled outside. If medicine could be made from a dog to treat a stomach problem, I would put the dog in the mouth of the beautiful small girl. And I would feel the life shining from her beautiful body; her dancing and singing. The meat of the dog would heat her cold and damp stomach up. The meat of the dog would absorb the poison making her sick.

But, that child was beautiful, not sick. Yes, she wasn't sick. Or, did her father think that beauty was a kind of sickness? Who knows? Perhaps that's how he sees it. Maybe she needs medicine for beauty.

Huh?

If so, then a dog is truly the only medicine. But why a dog? Where does this idea of a dog as medicine come from? The howling dog was heard once more. A howling which made the night seem as though it was dragging a corpse along the edge of the city.

Suddenly the door opened. The father of the daughter came in and embraced me.

"There is no medicine," he said. "There is no medicine for a stomach problem."

He bit my ear. Then he hurriedly took off all his clothes as if he was about to take a shower.

Was I a bathroom?

He tore off my clothes. Wrapped himself up in me

174

as if I were a towel. The howling of the dog reverberated from the lower floor, from under the ground,
from the middle of the earth. My navel exuded an
oily sweat. He fucked me as if he was stabbing a
dagger into the mattress. The howls of the dog could
now be heard from my navel.

My brow was wounded from his bites. Dog claws
emerged from the wounds. Flames came out of his
penis. Blue flames. Flames like tears. The flames
burnt my vagina. Metal and rocks began to melt.
Night was like an open coffin.

I could see a desire trying to give birth to a new
universe in the cavity of his mouth. My entire body
was entering that universe. A universe which emitted warm air and the sound of his child's singing.

Only my shadow remained outside, trembling on
the floor without me.

The girl who was sleeping suddenly convulsed.
Her hips rose, making her body form an arc. Her
muscles tensed. Suddenly an arseless bottle was
ejected from her stomach. The bottle flew out of the
window.

Then the child died; her beauty died.

I looked at the arseless bottle on my desk. The
howling dog was heard once more. As if the howls
came from my own thoughts. My mind was full of
dogs. I listened as intently as I could to those dogs
howling, as if listening to my own thoughts. Oh,
that's not what I meant. I listened as intently as I
could to my own thoughts, as if listening to dogs
howling.

Do you know what I mean?

What I mean is, I'm listening as best I can to every word you say. Every dark corridor in every sentence. Every corner and every comma. To every flame which inhabits every full stop and comma, every lie hidden between one sentence and the next. I will obey every lie until the banana tree beside my house burns down.

I gaze again at the arseless bottle on my desk.

I start to cry.

Tears which fall from within my thoughts.

A Person Born from Rain

I want to live in another person's body; in another person's reality. I know it's impossible. I know it's a falsehood I'm propagating. A cheap lie that turns a person into an object of embarrassment in his own kitchen, the sound of pots, plates, glasses and spoons causing an uproar.

But I continue to think about it. Every day. I feel it must be possible to fulfil that desire. It's impossible that I can't. That kind of transferral is something everyone should be able to do. I imagine that other body while turning on the electricity. Light suddenly illuminates a glass tube. When I turn off the electricity, the light goes out. It doesn't exit the glass tube. It dies. It is extinguished. Blood can pour from my body; sweat can pool on my skin. I think about it until the rainy season arrives. And all of those thoughts change, when the first rain truly falls in the front garden.

I stare at it from behind the glass. Suddenly the rain opens the door to my house, but it doesn't enter. It just stands before the door. Its body is a dense dark cluster of cloud. I can hear a faint sound coming from the cloud; like the dull whirring one hears in a plane. Since then, I've befriended the rain. I call it morning rain.

That morning, I was walking, holding hands with the rain. The air was cold. The wind made a curtain of rain. It was thin, fleeting, like a kiss on the neck before waking up in the morning.

"I've been waiting for you for a long time in that valley," I said. The rain didn't reply. It squeezed my hand as though feeling the passing of time.

"Counting time doesn't make humans interesting," it said. I stared at the rain. Its face was radiant. Its hair was neatly parted. Neat like tapestry woven from water.

"Time has never been able to touch you," I said. "You've never known age. You're always new. You've never lived in a body that grows to be an adult, and then old, and then becomes sick and dies. You've never felt sick, wounded or lonely."

The rain defended itself with the same old excuses. A thin blue light shone between the excuses.

"This is a special day for you and I," the rain said. "I've come from five miles away to meet you this morning. I've passed through valleys and forests, and crossed raging rivers."

"I truly wish you'd come to that valley last spring. The butterflies were dancing in the valley, the sun was dancing, composing my body from the leaves of beanstalks in the valley. But I realised it was impossible for you to meet me. It was also impossible for me to meet you. Fate had made it so. We crossed paths, but didn't recognise each other."

"Why are you trapped in language like that? It's as if you believe there exist things that cannot touch one another, that cannot know one another", it said. "We've never met because you hold such a belief. A futile belief."

As we descended the chalky slopes, the rain seeped into stones and gushed through pebbles. I gazed in wonder watching the stones absorb the rain. I was astonished to see the rain's aqueous architecture. The rain had made a space for dancing, turning a passive object into something dynamic. The rain animates, inviting me to dance once more with old memories. The rain knits together all events, letting the knitting seep into the soil, silently drifting past tree roots. The rain has an irreplaceable beauty that cannot be possessed. I know the rain is untouchable. I can't drip from branches nor seep into the soil. I'm separated by language and my body enclosing my world. The rain stares at me.

Its eyes are like hundreds of interwoven needles.

"I want to give you colour," I say.

"Any moment now, a rainbow will descend. It will make a thin circle, like the lines on a baby's palm. Butterflies will recognise the rainbow as their mother."

I clasped the rain's shoulder. Water dripped onto my palm. The sound of rain, falling on a stone, created a dense and rhythmic knocking. The heavy rain falling in my head made my eyes fill with tears, welling up from somewhere outside of me. As though my eyes were in another world, another world of tears. I knew my eyes weren't crying. There were no tears. I was sure there were no tears. My eyes convinced me over and over again, this is not rain, these are tears from outside of you. It was as if

179

my eyes had left my body in that valley, because they were so sure this is not rain but tears from outside of me. My body isn't stupid. It doesn't need to prove this is rain.

The rain patted my shoulder. Water poured over my bald head. "Hey, please, don't toy with me. Don't toy with my bald head with your rain. Don't toy with my heart and kidneys. You can't leak into my thoughts just because I have a bald head. Oi, don't muck around. I'll get rid of you with my head."

I took an umbrella out of my backpack. I also took out a raincoat and put it on. The rain dripped on my umbrella. The dripping sound gave me confidence that no danger would descend from above. The rain was falling heavily. I was sitting on a rock with my umbrella and raincoat. The leaves of the beanstalks trembled as the rain fell upon them. Their trembling created strange trails as fine waves pulsed towards my big toe. I felt as though I would leave my own body.

My body suddenly busied itself organising various things. I no longer trusted that I was indeed sitting down, wearing a raincoat and holding an umbrella. I no longer trusted my eyes and ears. But I realised my body couldn't escape. Something was stuck. My body didn't have an exit door. I tried to bust down the walls. The rain fell even more heavily and leaked through the pores in my skin. My body began to flood. I felt like my body was a dam about to burst. My body suddenly exploded like unravelling elastic.

I wiped the pieces of flesh from my pillow. Some

of the flesh was stuck to the mosquito net. Rays of light penetrated my bedroom window. The rain was waiting for me on the front veranda. We'd decided to go to a temple today.

I went out with my umbrella.

"Why are you using an umbrella?" it asked.

"Why can't I use an umbrella?" I replied.

"Because I feel like you're carrying a coffin on your head," it said.

"What kind of coffin?"

"A coffin for myself," it replied.

"A coffin for the rain?" I asked.

"Rain in a coffin," the rain asserted.

"This is just an umbrella," I replied. "It would be impossible to bury you in an umbrella."

"Your world is locked up in language," it said.

"No. Language is just words. Then sentences, then full stops and commas."

"No. You have both locked your worlds in language."

"What do you mean both of us?"

The rain took my umbrella, as if breaking the chair leg growing inside my head.

The rain hung from my palm. It fell and made a necklace around my neck. It hung on the bamboo leaves, making droplets on my veranda. Then we slept together in embraces of green. The leaves of the beanstalks in the valley, which made night from the sounds of insects, told a story about a flower that had never grown in that valley.

EPILOGUE:

Dinner to Conclude the Prose

There is meat curry. There is squid curry. Chicken curry. Jackfruit curry. Some meat with intense spices. Petai fried with ikan teri. Fried prawns. Sambal. Cassava leaves. There are yet more dishes on the table. This is the typical style of Sumatran Malay food.

The table is at a restaurant on Jalan Cikini Raya, in Jakarta, opposite the Taman Ismail Marzuki Arts Complex, in the midst of being renovated, along with the surrounding footpaths. The governor of Jakarta wants to reintroduce walking as a mode of transport in the city; a mode of movement that has become antiquated in the city. It's as though the lips of Jakartan roads are being prised open.

Andy Fuller invited us to dinner at this restaurant. We sit at the table where food is laid out like sacrifices for the gods. Andy's face holds a smile. It's as if he is returning to his childhood. I surmise that everyone presented with food he or she likes returns to their childhood.

Dinner always creates new stories. And this time I'm not the maker of those stories. I'm not good at making stories. Events, times, places, names, habits, relationships, in the process of writing prose, are never created out of nothing, but rather from the ruins of the past.

Nearing 63 years of age, I have only written 23 short stories, two novels and one collection of theatre scripts. Writing a short story is perhaps like meeting with a foreign planet on a strange orbit. Or a rare moment with a dead star. Short stories belong to an alien culture in this modern society living through the trauma of existing. The trauma inherent in the fundamental difference between the human and the non-human, male and female, dead and alive, black and white, god and devil: all of the academic categories we create in order to understand, but which soon enslave us. The trauma of our insanity in trying to accomplish something.

Encounters with unusual grey areas, where categories melt, tempt me to write some prose. When grey areas become irrevocably fluid, or categories harden in polarisation.

I experience the culture of prose as a difference between my expectations and the presence of a foreign body of prose, while I experience poetry as the practice of a mutant body. Modern society, whether in Indonesia or Australia, is growing as a mutant body in a digital ecosystem experiencing various waves of identity: it is looking for friendships in grey areas. Religion, which has a long and contested history since the fall of Sriwijaya, Pajajaran and Majapahit, is becoming stronger once more in Indonesia.

I thank Andy Fuller and his friends – Jorgen Doyle and Hannah Ekin – who have translated this collection of short stories for the first time. I cannot imagine the response of English language readers to my short stories. It is a response that masks, more or less, the principle of inter-literacy specific to literary texts. It is like eating Sumatran-Malay food served in a Sundanese style at this restaurant: something which I hadn't previously considered as an appropriate epilogue for this collection of short stories.

10th December, 2019, Jakarta

Afrizal Malna

Afrizal Malna

is an acclaimed poet, script writer, visual and performance artist and art critic. During the 1980s and 1990s Malna worked as principal playwright of the groundbreaking theatre group, Teater Sae. His poetry books include Abad Yang Berlari (1984), Yang Berdiam Dalam Mikropon (Jakarta: Medan Sastra Indonesia, 1990), Arsitektur Hujan (Yogyakarta: Yayasan Benteng Budaya, 1995), Kalung dari Teman (1998), Temantemanku dari Atap Bahasa (Yogyakarta: Lafadl Pustaka, 2008) and Pada Bantal Berasap (Yogyakarta: Omahsore, 2009). During the late 1990s he strayed from literature to document and work with the grassroots Urban Poor Consortium. Malna is also the author of a broad body of literary and cultural analysis. His work on Indonesian literature includes Sesuatu Indonesia (2000) and Pada Batas Setiap Masakini (Yogyakarta: Octopus, 2017), and his studies on Indonesian theatre are published as Teater Kedua (Yogyakarta: Kalabuku, 2019). Daniel Owen's translation of Malna's Museum Penghancur Dokumen (Document Shredding Museum) was published with Reading Sideways Press in 2019.

Jorgen Doyle is a translator, artist and gardener who has lived between Jakarta, Indonesia and Alice Springs, Australia since 2016.

Hannah Ekin is a translator, artist and library worker based between Alice Springs and Jakarta. Her translation of Afrizal Malna's short story, A Ruler to Measure Shadows, has recently been published in Exchanges Journal (Ohio, Spring 2020).

Andy Fuller founded Reading Sideways Press with Nuraini Juliastuti in 2017. He is based at Utrecht University where he is a post-doctoral research fellow with the ERC Consolidator Project, SACRASEC.

THE TRANSLATORS